Kona
Dreams

Kona Dreams

by
Shari J. Berman

Justice House Publishing, Inc.
Tacoma, Washington, USA
www.justicehouse.com

ACKNOWLEDGEMENTS

I would like to thank the many friends who read and proofread this novel. I wish to express my gratitude to Terry Browning for her technical assistance with the early drafts, and to Stephanie Elliott, Editor-in-Chief of JHP, for her invaluable input and suggestions on the final draft. Thanks to Robin for her encouragement and postproduction work, and to Shez for her dreamy pulp fiction cover art. I also want to thank my mother, who encouraged me not to use a pen name.

Kona Dreams is meant to be a light, fast-paced, erotic romance. The intention was that it be both fun and funny. While mainstream romance offers so much light reading, we have very little. Some in our community are stalled in the belief that we cannot have fiction without angst. I present this short work as an antidote to angst. It is my contention that not all lesbians are tragic characters; not all lesbians are twenty-nine; and not all lesbians are without an ounce of humor.

I also give thanks for my newly acquired hometown, overlooking Kailua-Kona, for its spiritual and physical beauty. Every day, I feel gratitude that the Information Age has allowed me to work and live in Hawaii. It is my sincere hope that those of you reading this will someday be able to visit all the places described in Kona Dreams.

Aloha and mahalo,

S. J. Berman

Spring 2002

I was sleeping, and you were sleeping too,
When our spirits left our bodies
And met where spirits commune!
We found each other and
Were lovers in a dreamscape
Who vowed to reunite when finally awake.

from "Dreamscape"
Kim Char Meredith

For Alice.

Alice no ka oe.

FREDDIE

"I'M TELLING YOU, FREDDIE," SUE punctuated the slight pause with an audible yawn, "you really could use a good woman!" The trials and tribulations of her cousin's love life had become predictable and boring, so Sue did what she could to steer the conversation in a more interesting direction.

"So you keep saying. What is this, Convert a Het Week?"

"Gee, let me look at my calendar…" followed by another yawn.

"What would I do? Run a personal: 'Frustrated Fred seeks willing Wilma'?"

"Works for me." Third yawn.

"I can take a hint. I'm terminally boring. Here I am, in one of the most gorgeous places on Earth, and I'm sitting in my hotel room talking to you." She could see that the sun was approaching the horizon and a romantic Hawaiian sunset was scheduled for the not-so-distant future. Maybe calling Sue was a bad idea.

"Are you still there?" Sue queried. She worked to stifle another yawn without much success, turning it into a combination yawn, snort, sniff and cough.

"Just trying not to interrupt the symphony of annoying sounds…"

"Gimme a break, it's almost midnight here." Sue sat up and shook her head. Her voice took on a firmer timbre. "Look, you call your middle-class dyke cousin late at night to help you out of the doldrums. You go on and on about how your second marriage has gone to hell, you say you're swearing off men, telling her you can't trust the bastards. What do you expect her to say? It's in the bylaws…Nicki is motioning for me to get off. I've got a deposition at 8:30 that's being filmed for a case out of state and I need to get my beauty rest."

"Sorry to keep you up, Counselor. And, yes, I know, you aren't that kind of counselor, anyway. Maybe I need to call Cousin Art to get my head shrunk." She stood up and dragged the phone over to the window to get a better view of the Kona sunset.

"Don't know about that. I've always had trouble imagining the world telling their woes to Artie. I guess I still see him as a sadistic brat holding frogs by one leg to watch them squirm," Sue said.

"Have you ever been in therapy?" Freddie countered. "I think it's a lot like squirming with some idiot holding you by one leg."

"Good one. Call me back if you need someone to handle the divorce."

"I thought you don't do divorces."

"I don't, but I've been in contact with this really sharp lawyer who volunteers some time and answers questions on the Lambda Legal Information page on the Internet. I'm pretty sure she mainly does divorce law. I think she's been involved in some high profile cases where a gay parent is looking at possibly losing custody based on lifestyle. Her name is Betty and she's in Southern California—matter of fact, she lives pretty close to your place. We've been sending a lot of e-mail back and forth. All of us lesbian lawyers are trying to stay networked. I've read some of her advice to people in trouble. She's good. I think you'd like her."

"Interesting story about her," Sue continued. "I understand that way back when, she was a housewife coming off of a lousy marriage. She fell in love with the female attorney representing her husband! After all the dust settled, they got together and Betty went to law school, too. Isn't that something?"

"That's something, all right," Freddie agreed. After another round of familial barbs and pleasantries, Freddie found herself sitting in the silence of her hotel room. Despite the stigma one might attach to her cousin's alternative lifestyle, Sue was easily the happiest person Freddie knew.

Freddie found herself thinking about this woman, Betty, falling in love with the husband's female lawyer. Betty was fed up with men and she did something about it. She switched brands. Freddie had never admitted to anyone that she herself had thought about what it would be like to make love to a woman. Was it that unusual? Didn't everyone have stray thoughts? Sue told her that when she was first coming out, every other person she told about her lifestyle mentioned some experience or family member or something along those lines.

Freddie played with the thought again for a moment. Stray thoughts were kind of fun. She recalled a scene of two women making love on a beach that she had seen in some plotless erotic film that Steve had rented. They had both voted that scene the sexiest one in the film and Steve had been particularly attentive to her needs when they had shut off the VCR and made love on the living room floor. That seemed like a lifetime ago.

She stood and opened the lanai doors. Paradise rushed into the room. The trade winds ruffled the curtains and the Pacific seemed to be washing in and out solely for her entertainment. She drew a ragged breath and felt a raw stab of pain. Beauty such as this was meant to be shared and here she was alone, poster child for lousy relationships.

She felt a different stab of pain—it seemed that even the unloved needed to eat. She had been to the luau the night before, and along with the Kalua pig, had ingested large constant reminders that she was not honeymooning or celebrating a milestone anniversary there. She opted to skip the suggested group activities that evening. She had scoped out a nice little Mexican restaurant overlooking the water. Perhaps all the other tourists would be thinking that they hadn't come all the way to Hawaii to eat Mexican food and she could share a little peace and quiet with some of the local crowd. She changed into a floral shorts ensemble, ran a comb through her hair, grabbed her bag and the room key and prepared to face the world.

Stephanie

STEPHANIE HOISTED THE BOX UP onto the counter. The clerk ran it through the postal computer and informed her that for five cents more she could send it Priority. The thought of making Jill wait a few extra days to pocket a nickel gave her a second of smug satisfaction. In the end, however, she didn't want to lose karmic points over a lousy nickel, so she gave the go-ahead to send the box Priority Mail.

Walking out of the post office next to Lanihau Center, she realized that she had effectively mailed Jill Foster out of her life. She leaned against her car and closed her eyes. The late afternoon held a warmth that was uniquely Hawaiian.

Jill still filled her thoughts, although her thoughts of Jill were none too pleasant. They had hoped to pump new life into the ailing relationship with the move to Hawaii, but while Stephanie had taken to the Aloha lifestyle like a dolphin to water, Jill had experienced an incredible homesickness for New York, and that had put the final nail in the relationship's proverbial coffin. Stephanie had joked to friends that it wasn't "homesick," it was "just plain sick" for anyone to prefer the filth and buzz of the Big Apple to the clean and calm of the Big Island. Jill had made some snarling zoo animal noise when she got wind of that comment. Stephanie had passed the point where Jill's opinion mattered and they spent their last few weeks together in open hostility. At that point, Stephanie, always the packer in the family, had agreed to forward a few boxes in exchange for taking over the house and letting Jill get back to her East Coast sanctuary.

A psychology professor of hers once said that the human memory was "like a Pez dispenser: the last thing in is the first thing out." Memories of relationships seemed to follow that pattern, as well. She was hard pressed to remember the sweet and romantic moments of their early years together. She could only remember bickering over small things and growing steadily apart.

The Kona Coast had been perfect for Stephanie in all ways but that one. She had taken gorgeous photographs. One of her photos had even won an award. Her on-again/off-again bouts with bronchitis were a distant memory. She had lost all of the nice pieces of art and fancy dishes in their ad hoc settlement, but she had assumed the mortgage and retained sole custody of Pepper, their five-year-old Silky Terrier. The bad news was that Pepper was the only one keeping Stephanie warm at night.

The oncoming evening brought a touch of melancholy. She lamented the break-up less than the loss of an "us." She wasn't very networked, and although she had numerous acquaintances, the only other lesbians she knew well were Nancy and Mary Ellen and Deb and Wendy, two couples who lived near Hilo. She didn't feel inclined to make the two and a half-hour drive to the other side of the island very often.

Dinnertime was fast approaching and she hadn't done any serious grocery shopping in days. She toyed with the idea of a fast food takeout window and decided to brave a real restaurant—something daring, spicy even.

She opened her eyes and as she was aiming the car key at the keyhole, she spotted a discarded lei on the low stone wall bordering the parking lot. The brilliant blue flowers were calling to her. She went to retrieve it. As she picked it up, several petals came off in her hand. She fingered the petals and used the lei for a round of "she loves me, she loves me not." As she broke off the petals, she repeated, "Mexican, Thai, Mexican, Thai" in her mind. The last bit of flower broke off on "Mexican." She went back to her car and headed to the Kona Cantina for dinner.

She Winked at Me, I Think

KONA PARKING WAS A TREAT, as usual. Stephanie drove up and down the rows and waited out someone who was just putting something in his car and didn't have the decency to wave her away. In the meantime, the guy who pulled in after her was smugly walking toward the waterfront. She circled around a few more times and finally found someplace to park "Honda-Honey," as she affectionately referred to her 1994 Accord. Negotiating a parking space off Ali'i Drive was one of the few exceptions to the usual Aloha spirit in her newly adopted hometown. She shook her head and shoulders to relieve the tension and allowed herself to predict what the specials might be as she walked up the steps of the Cantina.

Stephanie peered into the dining room from the bar area. "Hey, Steph." A chesty Island woman with long hair waved at her with one hand, serving tray in the other. So much for not knowing anyone. Momi's father was a manager at the local Honda dealership. He'd given her a great price on Honda-Honey, and over the past 18 months in Kona, she seemed to have been introduced to the whole family. She waited for the question. It came in Momi's strongest pidgin accent "Wheas yah friend? ...You folks always come her togedah, yeah?" As sweet as her local acquaintances all were, they weren't known for their tact.

Stephanie managed a choked chuckle that hinted at her embarrassment. She contemplated dodging the question, but decided to shoot it out of the realm of repeat performance. "Jill went back to the Mainland...for good." A nice finality to the statement. She fought hard to parlay the previous nervous chuckle into a casual who-gives-a-hoot smile, but she could feel the pain pulling at her eyes and mouth.

Momi, concerned at Stephanie's grave expression, pursed her lips and frowned. Stephanie's imagination went wild wondering what Momi must be thinking. Okay, there had been a few nights when they had first arrived in Kona. After several margaritas, she and Jill had snuggled in a back booth, held hands, and talked about things to buy for the new house. They had hardly kept their relationship a secret from the waitstaff at the Cantina. Momi broke the silence with: "I tink yah could do bettah. What is dat day say? ...Der're plenny fish in da sea!" She gave her a conspiratorial "girlfriend" poke and Stephanie sheepishly agreed with the analysis. Maybe not this particular sea, but there were plenty fish. "You need a margarita!" Momi had snapped back into her server language, which sounded much more like Standard English. "Frozen?" Momi asked as Stephanie glanced around for an open table.

"Yeah, frozen."

"You got it."

"Mahalo."

Stephanie chose a small table against the far wall, avoiding the back booths and their potential to trigger another mental stroll down memory lane. The place was more crowded than usual for a weeknight. She smiled at a local family. She spotted Doug Spears, the pharmacist from the Midwest, and Sumiko, his Japanese wife. Sumiko had placed in the amateur category of the photo contest that Stephanie had won. Much to her chagrin, Sumiko regarded Stephanie as some kind of photographic master and was extremely polite and deferential. Sumiko was still working on her English, so many of the ego-stroking descriptions of her respect for Stephanie's photos came via Doug's translations. The last time she had suffered from an ear infection, it had taken her an hour to get her prescription filled. Doug had insisted on passing on to her every nuance of Sumiko's praise for her work. She prayed that they had missed her entrance and the all-but-lei greeting from Momi, but when she looked up again they were beckoning her to their table. She reluctantly rose and went over to where they were sitting.

Sumiko pronounced her name "Sue-tephanie," which always made Stephanie smile. She spent several minutes chatting with them. They offered her a chair but she begged off, saying that she needed to work on some notes for a new project over dinner, so she wanted to be alone. Repeating the conversation in her mind, it sounded exceedingly lame, but Doug's many years in Asia had him politely nodding, almost bowing in unison with his wife. She further rationalized that they were almost through with dinner and she would have obliged them to stay much longer if she were to join their party at its denouement.

Upon returning to her table, she drew a long breath. Her fears of being out in public again had not exactly been allayed, but she had somehow passed a test. She was still reasonably adept at social interactions. Not exactly good at it, but she could get along.

There was ice sweat running down the side of her margarita glass and a small trail of salt had defected from the rim and followed the condensation. She coaxed the salt back up the glass and licked her fingers. She unwound the pink cloth napkin folded into the shape of a bird-of-paradise flower and wiped her hands more deliberately, then pulled out a pad of paper and made some notes for an upcoming shoot. After a few minutes, she felt that she had kept up appearances for the Spears. They weren't looking daggers, or would that be "spears," at her, as she had feared.

The margarita was starting to loosen the knots in her shoulders. She began drinking more leisurely. Her plan was to take the evening slowly, follow the drink up with a nice meal and some of the local coffee. She'd take a walk down the main drag, such that it was, and lose the margarita buzz before getting back behind the wheel.

At some point while she was lost in thought, Momi had dropped a menu on the table. She looked over the specials and closed it. Out of the corner of one eye, she noticed a woman alone at one of the back booths that she used to share with Jill. The woman was small with short blonde hair. There was something almost angelic about her face, beckoning Stephanie's gaze to linger far longer than she had intended. Their eyes met for a second, and as Stephanie began to look away it seemed that the other woman winked at her. Or did she? Matching shorts and top—probably a tourist. What would it be like to just have a one-night stand? Other people did it, or so they said.

The next thing she knew, Momi's apron was between her and the woman. Great timing, Momi. Her face red with a combination of anger at being interrupted and embarrassment at her shameless cruising, she avoided eye contact with Momi. Clearing her throat, she managed to order an appetizer of mahi mahi-filled mini tacos and an entrée of chiles rellenos in a flat tone. Momi glanced at her quizzically, and when Stephanie didn't look up or offer any explanation for the sudden chill in her voice, she went off to place the order.

She picked up her notepad once again and pretended to be looking at it as she stole another glimpse of the blonde. The other server, Jon, was placing several large platters in front of the other woman. An acute throb of disappointment hit Stephanie. Had she missed seeing someone else sitting at the blonde's table? A few minutes passed and nobody joined the blonde. Maybe someone was meeting her later and told her to go ahead and order. Stephanie doodled on the notepad.

Halfway through the appetizer Stephanie mustered up the courage to look back at the blonde. She was still alone. Hmm. She stifled a chuckle. Hearty appetite for a little thing. Mood improved, she doused the last mini taco in hot sauce and popped it in her mouth. A dialogue began in her head as to whether it had been a wink or a twitch. Something in her eye? She willed herself to think about something else; the inane debate over such a minute detail was like a weak episode of Seinfeld. Why couldn't she be the ballsy type? Her friend Joanie would have already had the woman's hotel key. However, Joanie lived in San Francisco. Wasn't there something in the water there that made everyone gay and fancy-free? Or was it something that made everyone gay fancy-free?

Contented simply to look for the moment, Stephanie shifted in her chair and glanced over again. Jon was placing Styrofoam containers on the table and scooping up leftovers for the blonde. Her throat constricted slightly. She really wanted to say something. Would it be that hard? She almost rose once and every fear she'd ever known kept her glued to the seat. Was the window of opportunity closing with her shy little fingers still on the windowsill? She rehearsed several things to say as the blonde passed her table to the exit. Nothing came out. The blonde spoke first.

"Hi."

"Oh, uh, hi."

Who is This Woman?

ALTHOUGH SHE WAS TRYING to avoid the "tourist thing," Freddie was nothing if not frugal. She had very neatly detached the coupon for free nachos from the coupon pages of "This Week Big Island" magazine.

As Freddie entered the restaurant, a strange shiver went through her. There was something familiar about the Kona Cantina. Déjà vu?

The server, who had greeted her at the entrance, was congenial and a bit too chatty. He told her she'd made a wise choice coming to the Kona Cantina; it was "really going on." He was intuitive, though. He had talked up their lanai seating, but was right there to contradict himself and sing the praises of the back booth when he noticed her look of pain when actually faced with the "going on" sunset view crowd. Peering out on the patio she had counted a handful of honeymoon couples and two groups of noisy Gen-Xers. Given that guest list, not unlike Garbo, she wished to be alone. *Screw the Kona sunset.*

They say you meet people when you travel alone, but instinct told her she didn't stand a ghost of a chance meeting anyone worthwhile on the lanai. Instead, she would have been bombarded by loud conversation, preventing her from enjoying any thoughts of her own. And it would soon be too dark to read a book if the eavesdropping possibilities were ruined by a prevalence of double digit IQs. Furthermore, those paying attention would have ended up pitying her either because she was a woman dining alone or because she ordered dinner as if she were going to the electric chair following the meal.

The server looked to be in his mid-twenties and of Asian descent. He went through the overplayed shtick, telling her, "My name is Jon and I'll be your server tonight." He pronounced server a bit like "sherver," but she had noticed this in other Hawaiians' English, as well. She thought the introduction almost comical, as he wore a badge that said "Jon" and had been the only one to interact with her. She wanted to tell him that she'd already read his name and that for having rescued her from the patio she would forever be in his debt, in which case they should both be on a first name basis and her name was Freddie. A female server called Jon away just as Freddie was teetering on the edge of teasing him. Left with the menu and a series of unused one-liners, Freddie settled back into the seat. In sharp contrast to the lanai, the inside of the restaurant was empty except for two men watching a game at the bar in the entrance area.

She thought back to her conversation with Sue again. The question repeated itself. Was a woman the answer to her woes? It certainly worked for her cousin. Sue and Nicki were one of those disgustingly happy couples that finished one another's sentences. When she had stayed with them for a week a few months earlier, she and Nicki had spent an afternoon shopping. Toward the end of the day, Nicki had confessed that she hated being away from Sue for so many hours. Freddie knew right there and then that Sue and Nicki had some connection that she had never experienced with another human being.

When "My name is Jon" returned, she busied him with stapling her coupon to the bill and relaying her drink order to the bartender while she had a good long look at the menu. After changing her mind several times, she decided to order guacamole, the chiles rellenos/shrimp tacos combination plate, and a Mexican Caesar side salad. At least half of it would taste all right cold. Why have that empty refrigerator in the hotel room, if not for leftovers? Determined not to let traveling alone cramp her style, she had ordered a full meal rather than the conservative dining alone alternative. A few nights earlier, a table full of jerks, obviously raised by wolves, had turned around to gawk at the large amounts of food being delivered to her table for one. It had made her extremely self-conscious and ruined her appetite. This time, she'd just offer anybody who stared an obscene gesture and be done with it.

Jon came back with the margarita and took the order. He shook his head several times and admonished her that their portions were large, but she prevailed. She tried to read her book while she was waiting, but her restless mental state resulted in going over the same two paragraphs three times. She returned the paperback to her purse and took several long sips. Okay, it was becoming a fixation. All mental roads led back to coming home in the middle of the day and finding Steve in bed with his secretary.

She'd yelled, she'd cried. She'd spouted Neil Simonesque invective, questioning why he couldn't have been more original than to have an affair with his secretary. She'd quickly enumerated any number of better partners with whom he could have been found *in flagrante delicto*. She had suggested the female phone employee who had refused to scale the telephone pole to fix their problems because of the ivy on the pole. Or the checkout clerk at the supermarket who was always eyeing him and giving him more coupon credits than the sale deserved.

"I would have felt better losing to such worthy opponents," she screeched. "But your secretary? You son of a bitch, you insult me!" It was a reasonable reaction, she had rationalized. Nobody wants to be a living cliché.

It was two weeks before her sabbatical. She had stopped back at the house because she had forgotten her checkbook and she needed to pay the balance for their trip to Hawaii. In that respect, the timing was good. She had paid the balance on hers and canceled his trip. Her agent, a divorced single mother, broke every rule in the book and refunded the initial deposit for Steve's fares.

The steel alliance of women scorned worked for her in spades. She hadn't meant to pour out her heart to a travel agent, but with no counselor or rabbi in sight, a travel agent seemed like the next best choice. Finding the right trip for clients took good people and counseling skills. Maddy had listened sympathetically, referred to Steve in terms that Freddie herself had thus far not vocalized and had managed, with just a few keystrokes, to kick Steve out of the computer and Freddie's life. In return, Freddie had extended her time in Hawaii and bought up a series of optional tours, including two weeks on the Big Island.

The napkin, which had started out a beautiful flower, was a patchwork of cheese grease from the nachos. She left a third of the portion on her plate. She practically swatted his hand when Jon offered to clear it for her. She'd gauge whether to eat or pitch the nachos based on the rest of the meal. She had an idea they would not make a good addition to the ample doggy bag she was planning.

As the nachos started to congeal and she grew antsy for the meal to progress, she discovered she was no longer alone in the main dining room. A tall, full-figured woman with chestnut-colored hair and huge eyes wearing a muu muu was being escorted to a table along the windows that divided the inside from the lanai. The same feeling of familiarity that had hit her when she walked through the restaurant crept over her again. Did she know this woman? She tried to get a closer look and noticed the other server was obviously a friend or the woman was a regular. Someone pushed through from the lanai to go to the restrooms, letting outdoor noise escape into the main dining room. Simultaneously, the background music seemed to grow louder, so her attempt to listen in on the woman's conversation failed miserably.

What was going on? Had she met this woman before? She often ran into people who had heard her lecture and remembered her. Had this woman been at a conference somewhere? No. It didn't follow. She was usually the one that people remembered. The woman couldn't be part of her tour group; it wouldn't make sense for her to know the restaurant personnel. She was overcome with strange sensations. A tingling began at the base of her spine and slowly crept up to her neck. The feelings were new, yet old and comfortable at the same time. Déjà vu? Wasn't this the cue for a few bars of the *Twilight Zone* theme?

The brunette had interesting coloring. Her face was pale, yet her forearms were tan. Did she drive a truck? Hmm…both arms were tan. Did she do some moonlighting in Tokyo? London—someplace where they drive on the opposite side of the road? Her imagination was way out in the offing, so she attempted to reel herself in. Maybe the tanned arms were from swimming. What difference did it make, anyway? Why did she care? The odd sensation, the feeling of familiarity, the pull towards this woman—it must be something else. Perhaps the nachos were digesting poorly.

The rest of the food arrived and she picked at each plate. Food seemed less important than it had just a few minutes ago. She picked up her book again as she munched a shrimp taco. This time, she couldn't even get through one paragraph. What was it about this woman? She put her book down and stole a long look. Maybe she was someone famous; she had the aura of someone special. Freddie willed herself to look away. After a long stretch of staring at her own fingernails, she looked up again. This time, it seemed as if the other woman was studying her. Their eyes met and Freddie could feel a series of involuntary movements throughout the muscles of her face. She was smiling, and the woman was smiling back.

She was acutely aware of the pulse in her forehead. She felt restless, nervous, intrigued, excited. Her emotional wires were charged. Always quick to rationalize, Freddie wanted scientific data to support and explain the jumbled network of emotions coursing through her. She submitted all the evidence she could muster to her internal CPU, and the retrieved analysis was *"sensation unfamiliar."*

She wasn't sure if it was fear of the unknown or just plain fear that propelled her out of the Kona Cantina. She had Jon packing up her food and running her credit card with only the tiniest bit of shrimp taco missing from her mega order. She had a plan. She would exit slowly, walking close to the woman's table, and then out through the bar. The woman would say something to her to explain how and where they had met or one of the guys at the bar would say something about "so-and-so, the famous thus-and-such" and point to the brunette. Her exit would clear up, once and for all, who this mystery woman was.

As she approached the brunette, she could see that she had huge intense hazel eyes with golden flecks. Her other features were soft in comparison. Their eyes locked for a moment. Freddie felt overwhelmed with questions. *Who is this woman? Why can't I breathe?*

Instead of explaining to Freddie who the hell she was, the brunette acted shy and tongue-tied herself. Some clever plan. The mystery woman looked to be counting on Freddie to say something first. With no time to devise something brilliant to say, Freddie settled on "hi," and the other woman sputtered a "hi" back.

She sensed there was more communicated in that exchange than in hour-long conversations she had had with other people. No, the brunette was not someone from a teacher's conference. She was fairly sure of that now. Her familiarity was something else. Something from a far away, untapped place. How many emotions can a person experience at the same time? All of a sudden this creature in a muu muu was the most daunting person on the planet. Now what? Standing with an armful of Styrofoam carryout boxes on her way to the door—there was nothing to do but leave.

Retraining herself in basic human propulsion, Freddie forced her rubbery legs to move one ahead of the other and managed to get out of the restaurant. She stopped when she was safe outside and stood with her back against the building wall. Her breath was ragged. All at once, she was very tired. Going out by herself had proven more strenuous than she had imagined. Gripping her take-out to her chest, she walked quickly back to the hotel. She filled the refrigerator with Styrofoam containers and got ready for bed. So what if it was only 8:05 in Hawaii, it was bedtime back home. She turned off the lights.

Midnight for Freddie

"DON'T MAKE ME KEEP REPEATING the question, just tell me how you knew," Freddie demanded. Freddie herself was fuzzy after the four-hour nap she had just taken.

"Geez, Freddie, it's six in the morning. Whatever happened to "Hello?"

"Hi, hello, how are you, greetings and salutations, up yours, now answer the question!"

"I don't know. I just knew. When I was twelve, I was the last piano lesson of the day at Mrs. Richmond's house. Her daughter, Lisa, came in as I was gathering up my sheet music and told her that Dad was coming home late. They were going to have dinner on their own. The next thing I knew, it was Mardi Gras. They were planning all sorts of fun stuff to do since Mom didn't have to wait on Dad. They invited me to the party. I started thinking, 'Wow. I can't wait until I grow up and my husband doesn't come home for dinner and I can be free and party...' A few years later, I realized that I didn't need a husband at all. I could just be free and party. I guess that's when I knew."

"Hmm."

"What's this all about, anyway? You meet Wilma?"

"I don't know."

"You don't know?" Sue sat up in bed and felt around the nightstand for her glasses. This was getting more interesting. She pulled the antenna up on the portable phone stand and started readying herself for the day. Her cousin's silence was communicating more than her words. "So, you met somebody? A woman? I told you so." More silence. "Hey, you aren't just messing with me, are you?"

"Stop asking me so many questions. I think I liked it better when I was boring you to death. I'm...I don't know, confused."

"Confused is good. It beats the hell out of self-destructive. I was afraid you were looking for another prick for strike three." She regretted the words the second they flew from her mouth.

"That was nice. Thanks. Just as long as I can always count on you to be supportive."

"I'm sorry, Freddie. You dangle this carrot in front of me and then you refuse to dish. There are those who kiss and tell and those who kiss and don't tell. But you, you're in a class all by yourself—you, who allude to things and drop small pellets of information and then leave me and my inquiring mind to speculate."

"When have I ever left the sordid details out when I'm talking to you?"

"Well..."

"Nothing happened, except my imagination jumped the track and I'm feeling out of control." It was Sue's turn to be quiet. "There was this woman in a restaurant last night. I had this strong feeling that I knew her from somewhere. I was looking at her, I turned away, then she was looking at me. It was more than a casual glance."

"Okay. So, did you talk to this woman?"

"Yeah. Sort of. I said, 'Hi.'"

"What did she say?"

"She said, 'Hi.'"

"How old am I going to be at the end of this story?"

"And then I walked out of the restaurant."

"You woke me up for this? Did Nicki put you up to this? This is a joke, right?" Sue could hear Freddie starting to cry at the other end. "Freddie? ...Freddie?"

"I'll talk to you later," she sobbed, and hung up.

Freddie pulled the covers over her head and continued to sniffle. Why did life have to be so damn hard? After the final episode with Steve, she had decided to shut down the relationship runway. It would be a snowy day in Waikiki before her heart would be soaring off for another disaster.

What, then? What was she to do? It had only been a short time since the split with Steve and she was feeling very alone. Although her marriages were not made in heaven, not being in a relationship was a much lower experience—purgatory, perhaps. Here in this honeymoon haven, however, it was pure hell. Maybe it was time for an affair. Couldn't there just be something fun, no strings, and no victims? Nobody had really piqued her interest recently, except...

Was she being unduly influenced? Her cousin had been telling her for a while that a relationship with a woman would solve all her problems. The world at large had her believing that such a relationship would just make life harder and messier. Sue insisted that this was the "coolest time in history to be a dyke." Was she really so easily persuaded? If she were a lesbian, wouldn't she have figured it out by now? She was more than four decades old, not a kid by anyone's standards. Nonetheless, flashbacks of the exotic woman in the muu muu made shivers run up and down her spine.

Many miles away on the East Coast, Nicki was sitting up in bed and watching her lover end the early morning phone call abruptly. In response to the quizzical look on Nicki's face, Sue responded, "I can skip breakfast. I just had a heaping helping of my foot in my mouth." Nicki chuckled her so-what-else-is-new chuckle and got up to make coffee.

Freddie tossed and turned, her overactive imagination in direct competition with a desire for calm and escape. The birds were beginning to sing when sleep finally won the battle.

Midnight for Stephanie

SHE STARTED AND FUMBLED to pick up the ringing phone. Conan's voice was now blaring from the tube, so she had slept at least an hour, as she vaguely remembered a political joke from Jay's monologue. She managed a sleepy hello as she hit the mute button.

"We woke you. Sorry. Deb told me I should wait until tomorrow, but I had to know. I'm picking something up, here. I get that she's not from the Islands. Yes, she's someone from the Madland. Damn, that's all I'm getting. Who is she? There ought to be a law about against leaving that sort of teasing message on someone's answering machine!"

"Look, Wendy, forget it. It's no big deal. I just wanted someone to talk to, and…"

"Sorry. Did the statute of limitations on this run out at 10:43?"

"10:43?"

"That's when the little man in our answering machine said you called. Just tell us what happened. And don't leave anything out. Deb is getting on the other phone."

"Hi, Steph," came Deb's smooth alto over the extension.

"Hi. I wish you weren't blowing this out of proportion. I saw this woman at Kona Cantina. She kept looking at me, I swear. I think she even winked at me once. She's this little tiny blonde. Cute. I mean, Kee—ute, like a grownup kewpie doll, but there's a really intelligent look about her. Probably a professional. Okay, so then, after ordering a truckload of food, she had it all packed up and got up to leave. She walked by my table and was waiting for me to say something. I froze. I had a chance. I know I did. But I looked at her like an idiot. She said, 'Hi.' I said, 'Hi.' And this very lame story ends there."

"Hmm…I'm surprised you didn't consider following her out," Wendy commented.

"I didn't think stalking her was appropriate. I usually don't do that until after the second date. Like I said, I froze. She might have been a tourist. I'll probably never see her again. She'll be my fish that got away story. She'll grow more beautiful and mysterious with each telling."

"You were right, you are an idiot," Deb offered.

"Oh, that's lovely, Deb. She's down, she's bleeding, and you're kicking her."

"I believe in tough love. First she lets that Jill creature use her like an Aloha mat and the creep moves back to the Mainland. Then, some sweet thing flirts with her in a restaurant and she lets her go. Does that sound smart to you?"

"She's right," Stephanie said, cutting off the crossfire between Wendy and Deb. "I'm an idiot. I don't seize the day. I don't seize anything. The last two relationships that I had fell into my lap and then fizzled out when I thought everything was going great and I couldn't be happier. I miss all the signs. Maybe this woman had something in her eye and on the way out she was just being nice. She might have thought I was somebody else. I hear I'm 'a type.'"

Stephanie continued on her downhill roll and Wendy eventually kicked Deb off the phone and tried to pump her back up. Wendy was a very spiritual person. She claimed to have premonitions about things that were highly accurate. "I have a strong feeling about this, honey. You haven't seen the last of your kewpie doll. Besides, Mercury is retrograde until the day after tomorrow. Don't expect any smooth communication until then. Now, go back to sleep. My little devil can't find the toothpaste; I've got to go."

"Bye, Wendy. Thanks."

"'Night."

Stephanie set the receiver down and smiled. Wendy and Deb were quite a pair. Deb wasn't really a devil, more like the devil's advocate. Wendy was a "good witch;" she had angelic moments, but she was a true yenta, wanting to put people together and always hungry for the latest gossip. The "kewpie doll;" it was a nice nickname. She could call her k.d. The rest of the crowd would think it had something to do with the singer. Her thoughts were interrupted by Pepper. She wanted one last outing before Stephanie retired.

The dog headed for a favorite spot in the yard. Stephanie hung back to gaze at the starry night. She loved the nights in Kona. She noticed a quick flash in the sky—a shooting star. She made a wish, and she suddenly felt happier than she had in months. She whistled for Pepper and they went back into the house. She locked the sliding door on the lanai and proceeded to turn out the lights and make her way back to bed. She watched a few minutes of a Sixties sitcom until she felt her eyelids getting heavy.

The Day After

FREDDIE AWOKE IN A COLD sweat. "A gluteus maximus," she said aloud, "I dreamed about someone's butt." She had never been good at remembering dreams in any sort of sequence; she tended to remember snippets. There was one overpowering image: Freddie's hands circling and caressing someone's naked buttocks. They were round, soft, and substantial alabaster cheeks with a faint bluish cast that glowed in the dark. So much for dreams always being in black and white. In the omniscient nature of a dream, she could see her hands wrapped around someone's behind and she could feel someone crouched over her at the same time.

She tried to recall Steve's body in her mind. Conjuring up a partial image, she began to scan down his backside in her head. His skin was darker than the person's in the dream; he was smaller and flatter. Definitely not him. She spent the morning fixated on the dream. She had never really understood all the hype about someone having a cute caboose, but there was something deliciously erotic about the person in her dream.

She wasn't as successful a vacationer as she had planned to be, so she decided to try getting some work done. She had a one-year sabbatical from the private high school she taught at to expand and revise the science book that she had published five years earlier. To mix business with pleasure, she had planned to include some information and photos about marine life and vegetation in Hawaii. She was even thinking of using some colorful Hawaiian fish to snap up the artwork on the cover. All things being equal, even teachers actually judged books by their covers. Put two reasonable textbooks side by side and the one with the snappy cover got the course adoption every day of the week.

She recalled seeing some interesting photographs in a gallery near the evil Mexican restaurant. She would brave that neighborhood again later in the day. She decided first to dust off the rental car, which had accumulated two days of tree gunk and flower petals. She was paying more than twenty bucks a day and had chosen to walk everywhere. It was time to venture off a bit farther.

Her first stop was Longs Drugstore at Lanihau Center, about an eighth of a mile from the hotel, for dental floss and cotton swabs. Progress.

There was something comforting about perusing the aisles of Longs. In addition to drugs, they had major sundries. She spent a long time in the homeopathic remedy section where she finally selected a detoxifying anti-stress tonic. She found special dog treats made by a Kona-based company and popped them in the basket for her neighbor's dog.

They had a substantial "As Seen on TV" section. She fondled the various defrosting trays and food sealers. She had become the queen of infomercials during the week after she threw Steve out of the house and could recite all the sales points of each gadget that she saw. The Defrost Wonders were cheaper than they had been on the infomercial and she toyed with the idea of getting one. Nah. Her microwave was the official defrosting device, and it wouldn't do to make any major appliance jealous. Nobody wants a food-nuker with an attitude.

∽ ∽ ∽

Stephanie revved up Honda-Honey and headed south. The toothpaste coupon expired today, so she needed to stop at Longs. She had thought about going up to the one in Keahou, but Ali'i was perpetually under construction and she had already come down off the highway to drop off a check at the Honda dealer. For a brief second, it felt as if the car were driving itself to the Longs at Lanihau Center.

Stephanie stopped at the coffee stand in front of the drugstore and ordered a small latte. She sat on a bench and sipped it. Despite the morning heat and the warm coffee, she shivered. She couldn't shake the dream. She remembered many of her dreams in great detail, but this one was particularly lurid. She was kneeling on the floor at the side of her bed. An unknown lover's legs were hanging over the side. She stroked and kissed her feet, her legs. She nuzzled the spaces between her thighs and her crotch. The woman sighed. She buried her fingers deep within this mystery lover and the other woman gasped with pleasure. She opened her mouth, parted her lips, and, just as she was about to partake of this wonderful creature, Stephanie woke up. The clock told her she had slept for hours, but she had felt groggy and deprived.

Longs had soy sauce on sale, so she placed a bottle in her basket. As she turned down the aisle to get the toothpaste, she caught sight of a blonde woman turning the corner and her pulse raced. Could it be k.d.? She hurried to the end of the aisle and looked both ways; only a little boy and his mother on the cross aisle. The blonde had gone left, so Stephanie went up and down and checked several aisles.

The woman left her basket in front of the cotton swabs in the baby product aisle and walked two aisles back to get some aspirin. Stephanie looked up the baby product aisle. There was an empty cart there. She continued on and cursed her luck. It probably wasn't k.d., anyhow.

Stephanie dropped a few new shots of flowers and marine life off at the Plumeria Gallery and chatted briefly with the owner, Marge Lau. They decided to have a particularly stunning shot of a school of Lemon Tang blown up. A few times a month, Stephanie stowed away on a snorkel cruise and took some underwater photos. She thought fish made wonderful subjects: intelligent, yet not demanding. The first time she had seen a group of Yellow Tang from the surface, it had reminded her of a bowl of egg yolks. They circled her and made her feel like part of the crowd. From that moment on, she had had a special affinity with these bright yellow members of the surgeonfish family with their majestic sail-like fins.

Marge gave her a small commission check for two photographs she had sold and Stephanie left her to talk to her photo lab about the enlargements. Tom would know the right size for the work; he had an excellent eye. As Stephanie pulled out of her parking space, someone in a white sedan pulled in. Glancing in her rearview mirror, Stephanie thought the woman looked a bit like k.d. This was getting ridiculous. Everyone looked like k.d. this morning.

❧ ❧ ❧

Freddie pulled the white Cutlass Ciera into the parking space. As the woman in the red Honda sped off, she had a fleeting sensation that she was the brunette from the restaurant. She shrugged off the thought and headed into the small plaza. She spent a half hour in the bookstore and a few more minutes looking at Aloha wear before she headed into the Plumeria Gallery.

She immediately found those wonderful fish photos that she had seen through the window and approached the gallery owner. Marge Lau listened to Freddie's author spiel and they exchanged business cards. Freddie felt somewhat embarrassed about her simple science professor/author card when she saw Marge's glossy gold-lettered number with the plumeria flower on the logo. She borrowed a pen and printed the hotel phone number and room number on the card. Marge Lau would be a good contact; she knew it immediately.

"You know, it's too bad," Marge commented. "You just missed the photographer. She stopped in with these prints a few minutes ago."

"These fish are fantastic! I think they'd be perfect for the cover of my book! I know they're some type of surgeonfish. Do you know what they're called?"

"Yellow Tang, sometimes Lemon Tang. The Hawaiian name is *lau-i-pala*. Actually, that was my nickname as a teenager because my last name is Lau!"

"How about this surgeonfish in the picture here?"

"I don't know the English name, but it's called *kole* in Hawaiian." The *kole* was brownish with a golden ring around its eye. It reminded her of the woman in the restaurant. "*Kole,*" she repeated.

"I need to talk to my editor, but I'd really like to meet with the photographer and discuss the details of obtaining rights for some of these. What's the photographer's name?"

"Stephanie Amalfi. Why don't I leave her a message and see if we can set up a meeting? What would be good for you?"

"My busy schedule?" Freddie laughed. "I'm here on vacation, more or less, so I can work around the photographer's schedule."

"Okay," Marge said and smiled. She flipped through her Rolodex and proceeded to leave a message on Stephanie's answering machine. Freddie browsed through the prints and photographs and decided to buy a poster of a seascape by a local artist. Fifteen dollars seemed like a bargain and she wanted to initiate a patron relationship with Marge. It was a small price to pay for an introduction to a local photographer.

Freddie made her way over to the ice cream parlor down the block from the gallery. She munched a scoop of Kona Coffee Crunch and took in the network of tourists and local people that came in and out and walked by. Business died down a bit and the teenage boy who had served her sat down in one corner and proceeded to nod off. A balding older man came out of the back room. "Kimo," he barked, "get off your *okole* and get back to work."

She took in this new information with interest. A chuckle worked its way from the back of Freddie's throat. The fish that reminded her of the woman in the restaurant was a *kole*. The dream came back to her in vivid detail. Had her dream been about Kole's *okole*? What was happening? The world as she knew it was being turned on its ear—or, more appropriately in her case, on its butt.

〜   〜   〜

Stephanie let Pepper have the run of the yard while she checked her answering machine. The message from Marge sounded important, so she speed-dialed her immediately. She cradled the portable between her ear and shoulder as she stepped out onto the lanai and snapped her fingers for Pepper to return. Pepper was distracted momentarily by a colony of ants. She snapped louder and hissed, "Pepper, get your *okole* back in here." Marge picked up on the fourth ring and must have heard the last four words.

"Hello?" Marge offered in a surprised and questioning intonation.

"Hi, it's Stephanie. I was just yelling at my dog, sorry. So, who is this new client?" Pepper finally acquiesced and tracked mud into the house.

"Actually, she's a science teacher who wants to use some of your photos in a textbook…"

Disappointment washed over Stephanie. Textbooks usually meant low or non-existent fees. She'd been there before. "Okay," she started with much trepidation, "What would be involved?" The bills were piling up faster now that she was paying the mortgage by herself. A little sale was better than nothing at all.

"She'd like to meet you and talk about it. I think she may want to commission some shots."

Great. She was going to call the shots, get Stephanie to do extra work, and want to get the photos for ten cents on the dollar. She already disliked this science teacher. "When does she want to meet?"

"She said that could be at your convenience."

Well, that was more like it. "Is tomorrow at 11:00 okay with you, Marge?"

"Perfect. After your meeting, I'll take you both to lunch. My treat."

"By the way, what's her name?"

"Winifred Shapiro...Ph. D."

"Thanks, Marge. See you tomorrow." She clicked off the portable phone. Winifred Shapiro? Give me a break. Nobody would name a kid Winifred Shapiro. And a title, no less. The only "fudd" she had any time for was Elmer. Stephanie had an MFA in photography and she'd known Marge for almost a year. Had her degree ever come up in conversation? How did Marge know this woman had a doctorate? Had she dropped it in conversation? Did she introduce herself: "Hello, darling. My name is Winifred Shapiro...Ph. D, you know...but if you kiss my ass, you can call me Winnie."

Okay, she was in a bad mood. Despising this woman on principle was going a bit overboard. She prided herself on at least trying to be fair. She would wait until tomorrow and let the woman actually give her a few dozen reasons to hate her guts.

Good Bath Gone Bad

STEPHANIE LEANED HER HEAD BACK against the tile above the bathtub. It had probably been years since she had taken a bath instead of a shower. She had briefly soaped up and showered off Japanese style before filling the tub. She had used some bath beads and was soaking in the slightly oily, soapy solution. She used a washcloth to rub the suds over her neck, shoulder and the tops of her breasts. She thought back to the early days when she and Jill had bathed together. Getting over a relationship seemed to go in phases similar to mourning a death. She'd been through it: shock and denial, anger, bargaining, depression, and acceptance. She now was passing into a new phase, the restoration of libido.

For weeks on end after breaking up with Jill, she found the thought of physical contact with another human being repulsive. She had caught a glimpse of Wendy and Deb in an embrace and had felt true waves of nausea that transcended old-fashioned jealousy.

She had a book and a magazine along with a cool drink and the portable phone outside the tub. She was set for a long leisurely soak. She drifted into one of her favorite fantasies—making love on a small boat on the ocean. As she squeezed the warm bubbly water from the washcloth and let it drip down between her breasts, she imagined her head resting on the side of the boat. A faceless lover was circling her nipples with her tongue and trailing exquisite nails down her back. The warm water and the fantasy caused her to arch her back and breathe a bit erratically. She started to reach for herself when the phone blared out an angry ring. Who the hell could it be? She rubbed one soapy paw against a towel above her head and engaged the phone midway through the third ring.

"Hello...?"

"Hello."

The voice was deep, sexy, and vaguely familiar. More than she expected from the untimely interruption.

"Is this Stephanie Amalfi?"

"Yes."

"Oh...hi...this is Winifred Shapiro..." So much for being familiar. Is 11:00 not convenient for the science diva?

"Oh...uh-huh."

"Am I catching you at a bad time?"

Yes. I was about to masturbate and forget that I don't have a lover or much of a life at the moment. "No...Marge said that she was going to arrange a meeting for tomorrow morning."

"Yes. I'm just thrilled. I'm so looking forward to meeting you."

Saying the feeling was mutual would be too big a stretch.

"Uh...thanks."

"I was wondering if you could bring along any other fish or fauna photos that you happen to have on hand...if it wouldn't be too much trouble."

"Sure." Really. Fish or fauna. Who talked like that? Only someone named Winifred. She did have that sexy voice, though. She probably had the kids in her classes paying attention to more than "fish and fauna" when she spoke.

"Well, you have a pleasant evening, now. I'll see you tomorrow."

"Oh, yes. Thank you." She knew that if she concentrated she'd be able to locate her manners. "I'm looking forward to our meeting, too."

"Bye, now."

"Goodbye."

〜 〜 〜

Freddie put the phone down. Ms. Amalfi wouldn't win any awards for warmth, she mused. Marge had mentioned she was from the East Coast. Maybe she had one of those posh eastern pedigrees that included the mandatory stick up one's arse. She was looking forward to meeting the photographer, nonetheless. She thought that she could get a photo for the cover and three or four inside photos in the deal. She'd talked to her editor and had a ballpark budget with which to make an offer. Thinking back to the first edition, that photographer had been a pain in the ass, too. Maybe it was par for the course. Good photographs would perk up the second edition. It felt wonderful to be thinking about something other than her three-second encounter with the golden-eyed brunette.

≈ ≈ ≈

Stephanie let the water out of the tub and cursed. She just knew that Winifred Shapiro, Ph.D., was trouble. Nice voice, but trouble. And the nerve, interrupting her once-in-a-blue-moon bath. She thought it might be a good time to take some of the lesbian erotica out of the closet. She was up for a good sexy read.

Business Lunch

It was 10:52. Freddie entered the gallery just a bit early. Nobody seemed to be there. Then, she heard voices coming from the office in the back and headed in that direction. The door to the office was open and Marge nodded to her. The artist was hunched over a desk, shuffling through a stack of framed photographs. She was wearing light peach-colored cotton slacks. Bent at the waist, it looked as if the ice princess were mooning the gallery.

"I know there's a night shot of a parrotfish in here somewhere," Stephanie grumbled as she rummaged through the stack.

"Winifred Shapiro, I'd like you to meet Stephanie Amalfi."

Stephanie straightened up, her face colored from bending over the photographs. She made eye contact as the good doctor gasped. She could feel the blood quickly draining out of her face and the pulse in her forehead go into overdrive. Stephanie was the first to recover the power of speech. "Dr. Shapiro, how do you do?"

"Please, call me Freddie." She offered her hand. Stephanie took the kewpie doll's delicate hand in her own large one. She held it much longer than was socially acceptable and Marge looked away.

There was a pregnant pause. Stephanie looked at her kewpie doll. She was dressed in a red print blouse and baggy black shorts. She couldn't help thinking how easy it would be to get an entire arm all the way up one of the legs.

"I need to take care of the front displays. Go ahead and use this office. I'm sure you two have a lot to discuss." If only she knew.

Freddie produced a business card and Stephanie managed to get one of hers out of her bag feeling as if she had grown several extra thumbs. Stephanie saw the "Ph.D." and realized that was how Marge had known the author's title. *Damn, she's the cutest professor I've ever seen.* She found the nerve to go first.

"My friends call me Steph."

"As opposed to 'Phanie'?" Freddie pronounced it "fanny." They laughed, a tense, quasi-maniacal laughter. Freddie didn't bother to mention that she had been stockpiling buttock jokes for the past 36 hours.

"Uh...you don't look like a Shapiro," Stephanie offered.

Freddie's eyes darkened. An anti-Semite? "Actually, I was a Berkowitz and I married a Shapiro; I can show you the horns..."

"No, no, I didn't mean..." Stephanie shot back, horrified. "It's just that... You know, I'm half Jewish, myself... and."

Easily threatened. Interesting. Much more vulnerable than she appeared. "Which half?" Freddie asked.

She managed a short chuckle, but Stephanie turned beet red.

What? Freddie remembered a guy she knew in college who had an Italian mother and Jewish father who used to claim that he was Jewish from the waist up and Italian from the waist down. Surely she didn't think that Freddie was implying something like that! "I meant..."

"I know what you meant. My mother is Jewish. I don't know of any Jewish Amalfis, although there are some rumors that my father was from an old Jewish family that converted to avoid persecution." Stephanie straightened up, happy that some semblance of ability to articulate had returned. As the kewpie doll attempted to digest the information, Stephanie continued. "I just had this picture of Dr. Shapiro as someone with wild gray hair, granny glasses, a large sculpted nose—sort of a cartoon witch with an education."

Freddie was about to lecture this woman on her narrow-minded stereotypes when she glanced up. The golden-flecked eyes were unhinging her and Stephanie's mouth was slightly ajar in an amused grin. Rather than criticizing her, she offered more information. "I'm actually in the process of extricating myself from the Shapiro clan, " she whispered. "After the divorce, I haven't decided whether or not to change my name professionally. The first edition of my book sold well and my editor has expressed a preference for having the same name on the second edition."

Stephanie searched her eyes. Was she looking for a quick roll in the hay with a dyke to forget her failed marriage? Was the marital status an invitation for Stephanie to get down and personal?

As terminally cute as Stephanie found this sweet little thing, her values sucked. She'd bought into the patriarchy full tilt and gone as far as changing her name. She'd mentioned her marital status twice in this short conversation. Society looked at divorced women much differently than unmarried women. This woman had never had the various labels to deal with that Stephanie had taken on as an admitted gay woman. Every muscle in her body was in a knot. One side of her wanted to get naked with Professor Shapiro right here in the gallery office. The other wanted to smack her upside her male-identified head.

Freddie had a deep ache from the pit of her stomach pulling on to points south. Perhaps she was indeed turning queer. She just wanted to touch this woman. Surely she could forgive a few stereotypes. She patted Stephanie's hand, smiled devilishly, and said, "Why don't you show me what you've got?"

Stephanie grinned and replied, "You'd better be talking about my photos."

Instinctively, they edged away from one another in order to muster up the discipline to spend the next hour talking business. Freddie indicated there were several chapters for which she could use Stephanie's pictures. In addition to fish, Stephanie showed her photos of plants and birds, as well. Stephanie was pleasantly surprised to find that the publisher might be offering real money. It was a larger publishing house than she had worked for before, and the rough figures Freddie quoted sounded fair.

The conversation was even and focused. Eye contact was kept to a minimum, as it caused them each to look away with discomfort. Freddie felt as if the room were magnetized. If she dared to look into this woman's eyes, she would be pulled over and would fall in.

Stephanie noticed that Freddie was having trouble looking at her, too. When Freddie was looking down or away and explaining something, Stephanie found her eyes wandering to the peek of cleavage where the floral blouse was buttoned. She had the urge to drop something on the floor for Freddie to pick up and chided herself for thinking like a teenage boy plotting ways to see more cleavage. She cleared her throat self-consciously and turned her watch around to see the time.

"What a great watch! I thought it was just a bracelet," Freddie commented.

"Oh, you like it? My…a friend gave it me for my birthday. She's a jewelry designer."

"Oh, it's an original?"

"Yeah, I guess so." She twisted the watch again and moved it a bit higher on her arm so that it would stay in place. It had a smallish face and large silver bracelet clasps designed to cling to the wrist. Now that they had talked business, an odd silence had set in. *I wouldn't have to do anything else*, thought Stephanie. *I just want to kiss her. That would be enough.*

Marge popped her head into the room. "Ready for lunch?"

"Yeah," they said in unison. Everyone laughed and they filed out of the room and walked through the gallery out into the late morning sun.

Lunch with Marge took place at a small Thai restaurant. Marge had insisted that her "guests" sit side by side on the comfortable cushioned bench while she sat in one of the wooden chairs opposite.

Freddie had gotten in first and sat next to the wall. Someone sat down at the next table and Stephanie moved closer to Freddie. The situation would have allowed her to sit farther away, but the heat from Freddie's arm began to warm her all over and she was unwilling to give it up. It seemed that Freddie had a few inches between herself and the wall and she noticed that Freddie hadn't moved away. Stephanie spoke very little and listened to Freddie's voice. She wanted to close her eyes. She was almost certain that if she were ever in the situation where Freddie was reading her a bedtime story, she could come just listening to her voice.

Throughout the meal, Freddie kept checking her plate and seeing that almost none of it was gone. Stephanie was practically sitting in her lap. Was this what it was like to be attracted to a woman? She kept having to remind herself to breathe and her coordination was almost totally useless. At one point she had started to drop her fork and Stephanie's hand was there to catch it. Her arm had casually brushed Freddie's breast. Freddie could feel her nipples straining at the cups of her bra. Her throat was totally dry. All the moisture in her body seemed to be gathering in one place.

Marge looked at her watch. "I need to go back to the gallery. Why don't you two take your time? I'll see you later." She handled the check with the server and they said their good-byes.

Stephanie made no move to peel herself off of Freddie. Instead, she slipped off one sandal and began to run her toes and the side of her foot over Freddie's calf. Freddie responded with a gasp and a hiss.

Stephanie twisted her watch back into view again. It was 1:30. The late lunch diners were all speaking Japanese. Their server had had barely enough English to take the order and was nowhere to be seen. Perhaps it would have been more prudent to discuss the textbook and photos further, but it was the last thing on her mind. She felt no need to be too discreet in this crowd of non-English speakers. Stephanie uttered a small prayer and began in a soft, steady tone, "Have you ever been with a woman?"

"No," Freddie answered in a very small voice.

"I've been with several. I even thought I was in love once or twice. Maybe this is just physical, but I have never felt anything this strong in my entire life."

"Me, neither." It was barely audible.

"Until about five seconds ago, I believed that I wouldn't touch a dyke-virgin with a ten foot pole. Also, I make it a policy to have a strong intellectual relationship with any potential lover before we take it any further."

Freddie nodded wondering how long it was possible to hold your breath before passing out. She finally blew out a breath, compelled to respond. "I agree."

"But, if I don't have you alone in the very, very near future," Stephanie continued, "I'm going to explode and embarrass the ever-loving hell out of both of us."

Freddie agreed with that as well. Freddie found her voice, and although it was still low, it was much clearer than it had been for the last few seconds. "My hotel room is just a short walk from here."

"I promise to be gentle."

Round 1

THEY WERE SITTING IN FREDDIE'S room. The walk over had slowed the pace a bit and allowed the intensity to dissipate ever so slightly, enough so that spontaneous combustion was no longer imminent. The room had an interesting design. There was a small bed with large pillows to convert it into a sofa during the day and a king-size bed across from it. Stephanie sat on the couch-like thing with Freddie across from her on the big bed. Freddie had poured them each a glass of white wine from a bottle she had opened the night before.

For the calm, rational, conversational portion of the day, they discussed safe sex. At this point, Stephanie sounded more like the science teacher than Freddie.

"Since this is the 90's, I think we should have a little chat about STDs."

"STDs?" *Weren't they a radical group in the 60's?* Freddie thought.

"Sexually Transmitted Diseases!" Maybe she wasn't really a science teacher and she was targeting lonely and horny woman. "Statistically, sex between women tends to be less of an issue vis-à-vis most of your sexually transmitted diseases, but I don't plan to be one of those fraction of a percentage statistics. There are devices that we can use to be safe. Of course the safest thing would be to know…"

Freddie raised her right hand. "I've had sex with a grand total of three men in my life." She put her hand down and went on. "The boy I lost my virginity with claimed to be a virgin himself. He was appropriately awkward, so I believed him. That was 22 years ago, so the likelihood of his having passed on any diseases to me that have gone heretofore undiscovered is relatively small."

Although there was a great deal of defensiveness in Freddie's voice; this was the bedtime story Stephanie craved. Hearing Freddie tell the story of her life was causing a deep throb between her legs.

"My first husband and I broke up because we ended up boring each other to tears. During most of our marriage, he was very religious and would have believed he deserved some biblical punishment had he thought to have an affair. Although he accepted that I was from a less religious background, he followed many of the Chassidic practices. Toward the end, well after any sexual relationship existed between us, he had some kind of reversal of faith. He still went to the synagogue every Friday, but he lost the coat, hat and beard. When he shaved his beard, he had the worst attack of narcissism I have ever had the misfortune of witnessing. In his eyes, I paled next to his new, clean-shaven reflection. I understand he's still single. I guess he could never find anyone he loved an eighth as much as himself. I had a postcard from him about a year ago. He had quit his job as a pharmacist and was trying to break into show business."

Even if she was making this up, it was a pretty amusing story.

"That brings us to Steve Shapiro, my soon-to-be ex-husband. We haven't had sex since we both had too much to drink at a party about ten months ago. I know that it is unusual to go that long, but we were each involved in our careers and I stopped thinking about it. I had this trip to Hawaii planned as a second honeymoon. On the day I was supposed to pay for our tickets, I stopped home unexpectedly to pick up the checkbook. He was wrapped around his secretary on the sofa. The honeymoon was starting without me. The secretary had only been working there for two months. She replaced a woman who was retirement age. He swore up and down that it had only been going on for two weeks. He said he was planning to end it. I told him to tell it to the judge."

She noticed Stephanie looking at her raptly and continued. "I work very closely with the local Red Cross. I donate blood on a regular basis and some of my students volunteer there after we do the unit on blood-typing. As of a blood screening I had last month, I am STD-free." Finishing her speech, she gestured grandly at Stephanie to indicate that it was her turn.

"Okay. I had a few feel-around-and-pant-a-lot relationships with men when I was in college. One guy and I got pretty tight and had oral sex. The year I graduated, my longtime roommate and I experimented a bit with the lesbian thing. She decided that she needed a penis in her life, so I was left by the wayside. It wasn't too much longer before I realized that I needed everything but a penis in my life." Stephanie cleared her throat and looked at Freddie. Freddie was frowning in sympathy.

"I moved to New York and had two short relationships with healthy women who had little more experience than I did. Then, I met Jill. Jill had been in a ten-year relationship with a woman who died of cancer. As far as I know, that was the 'love of her life.' Or maybe the relationship was romanticized and her dead lover canonized in retrospect. In any event, the whole time we were together, she seemed to be searching for the perfect place, the perfect job, the perfect orgasm, and it all kept eluding her. Idiot that I am, I thought if I hung around and was more loving and more committed, that we'd live happily ever after and Jill would be satisfied with life." This was fun. Now they were both depressed.

"Jill was one of those people who almost always got her way," Stephanie continued. "Coming to Hawaii was the first, and last, big thing we ever did that was my idea. Jill's a jewelry designer, and fairly successful. She could send in drawings and samples from wherever she was and didn't have to be at some office from nine to five. I figured we could live anywhere and I knew that Hawaii would be good for my career and my well-being. It was good for my career, all right, but it cost me the only long-term relationship I ever had. Jill got tired of Hawaii really fast. They call it 'rock fever.' She expected me to go back with her to the East Coast. When I objected, she offered me my walking papers." Stephanie was fighting back tears.

Freddie moved over and sat next to Stephanie. She patted her knee gently. Stephanie put her arm around Freddie and Freddie leaned her head against her shoulder. Stephanie suddenly felt shy. She pressed her lips to Freddie's forehead giving her little feathery busses that could not be too overtly interpreted as kisses. Her mouth moved closer to Freddie's. Freddie closed her lips over Stephanie's and made the first move. Stephanie had steeled herself for a chaste kiss, but Freddie probed and gently slipped her tongue into Stephanie's mouth. Stephanie gasped. As they came up for air, Stephanie queried, "Where did you learn to kiss like that?" In response, Freddie offered a throaty giggle.

Assuming that everyone had been telling the truth, neither of them had had scads of sexual partners. Rather than going out to hunt down dental dams or using the shower cap, they decided to trust one another. Somewhere in her tossing and turning the night before during the wild dream about an obviously female derriere, or her panting at having this woman's shoulder pressed up against hers during lunch, Winifred Shapiro had decided that she was going to take the lesbian plunge.

Locked in an embrace, they moved over to the bigger bed. Freddie grabbed the curtain guide from the edge of the bed and darkened the room. They rolled around, kissing and nuzzling one another's necks. Freddie stuck her tongue in Stephanie's ear and Stephanie squealed. They gently probed the inside of each other's lips until their tongues met to dance together in a steady rhythm. The serious discussion had cemented the idea that they were indeed to become lovers, and a tacit agreement developed to slow down and explore one another thoroughly.

Freddie had never known kissing to be this erotic. They were still clothed, but had trailed their tongues down the crevices between each other's breasts. Stephanie untucked Freddie's blouse from her shorts. It was apparent that the action was about to escalate. Suddenly, Stephanie backed away unexpectedly and said... "Oh, my god, I forgot about Pepper. I have to go home."

Freddie experienced a blinding anger. Pepper? Had Stephanie told her about all past lovers and conveniently left out her present squeeze? The only person she had ever heard of named "Pepper" was the slinky little policewoman on television.

"Pepper?" she asked, trying desperately to keep her voice even.

"My dog. I'm sure she's crossing her paws by now. Come on. We'll have dinner at my place."

Freddie was flooded with relief. It wasn't until they started down the hallway that they looked at one another. They quickly rushed back to the room and tucked and smoothed their clothing and brushed their hair. Freddie decided that if she were going to come out of the closet, she'd prefer to look like something out of a dry cleaning bag than something rumpled off the floor.

Rounds 2 and 3

THEY WALKED TWO BLOCKS TO retrieve Stephanie's car from behind the gallery. It was red and looked as if had been recently washed. Freddie pointed to a decal of a honeybee on the back window. "That's cute."

"Thanks. I always called this car 'Honda-Honey,' so Jill got that sticker to put on the window. Funny how you've noticed all of Jill's little presents to me!"

"Seems like we have similar tastes."

"Touché."

They continued to chat amiably for the fifteen minutes it took to get to Stephanie's place. Their conversation was desultory, touching on topics as diverse as the locations of black, white and green sand beaches on the island to volunteer literacy programs. Perhaps they had other things in common besides a burning physical attraction.

They had been heading east, straight up Palani Road. Stephanie turned off onto a smaller street and drove a few hundred yards further, finally pulling up to a freshly painted little bungalow that sat at an elevation of about 1500 feet overlooking Kailua Bay. It was a clear late afternoon and there was a spectacular, albeit distant, view of the ocean.

They stood outside for a few minutes and talked about the view and the neighborhood. "Sometimes we get wild animals up here."

"Wow. I'd sure love to see that."

"And the sunsets...they defy description."

There was a muffled whine coming from the house. Stephanie

chuckled and unlocked the door to the house. Pepper wanted to check out the guest, but nature was calling in a rather loud voice. Both women followed the dog through the house and Stephanie unlocked the door to the lanai. As Pepper scampered beyond the patio to the edge of the yard Freddie lowered herself into a lawn chair. Stephanie disappeared and soon reappeared holding a tray with two glasses and a pitcher of iced tea. An afghan was draped over her shoulder. After setting the tray down on the patio table, she tossed the afghan to Freddie. "It gets cold up here, you may need this." Looking into Stephanie's gold-flecked eyes, Freddie had a hard time imagining being cold. Pepper came over with a gummed up tennis ball in her mouth.

"Don't you have a nicer toy than that, Pep?" Stephanie asked. Stephanie had changed into what they always called "something more comfortable." The peach slacks and silky blouse were gone and she was wearing a long sundress, not unlike what she had on that night at the restaurant.

"I don't mind your tennis ball. Come here. You aren't one of those wild animals she was telling me about, are you? Look at you. Aren't you a pretty Silky? Who does your hair?" Pepper was duly impressed and rolled over in response to Freddie's cooing voice.

Stephanie was flabbergasted. Nobody ever got Pepper's breed right the first time. They either thought she was an overgrown Yorkie, or they made some rude comment about her being one of those "little yappy things." She started to comment, but there was some serious bonding going on between Pepper and their guest. Pepper snapped back onto her feet and picked up the ball. She shook it vigorously from side to side and then offered it to Freddie. Freddie wrested it away and tossed it to one corner of the lanai. Pepper retrieved it and they repeated the process five or six more times.

Stephanie finally interrupted with, "Hey, I thought I was the one that was going to get spit all over you."

She didn't mince words. Freddie took in a breath and replied, "Well, Pepper sure is getting a lot of attention today. I thought she was the lover you forgot to mention and she thinks you brought me home as her playmate." She continued, growing more daring, "Why don't you bring one of your toys over here and let me have at it?"

Stephanie didn't have to be asked twice. She lifted Freddie's supple legs and straddled the lawn chair. She brought them down so that they landed around her waist. She held Freddie's face and kissed her passionately. This time when she moved along her neck, she unbuttoned the first few buttons of Freddie's blouse. Freddie's breath was hot and rapid against her cheek. "Do you have neighbors?" Freddie questioned in a hoarse whisper.

"Nobody close enough to hear what I'm going to do to you...so don't bother crying for help." Stephanie quickly had the rest of the buttons undone and the blouse strewn across the table next to the drinks.

Once more, Freddie's nipples were straining against her bra. Stephanie was slow and deliberate. She kissed the top part of her breasts that peeked out of the bra. She bit at her nipples through the nylon. Freddie's nipples kept getting harder and harder. Freddie was convinced she could have cut diamonds with those nipples. When she thought she would die if Stephanie didn't free her aching boobs, Stephanie lowered one strap down her shoulder and exposed her right breast. She drew her nipple in her mouth, held it in her teeth and sucked in the air around it. It was like being touched with icy air. What she thought was maximum hardness was surpassed by something even tauter.

Freddie clasped her hands around Stephanie's waist and pulled up the back of the sundress. She gasped as she felt Stephanie's bare behind. "I didn't mean to shock you," Stephanie said, almost apologetically. When I went to change, I noticed that my underwear was..." Freddie inhaled her mouth before she could finish the thought. She then let Stephanie kiss her breast again and she guided her head with one hand, fondling Stephanie's bare bottom with the other.

Stephanie stood up suddenly. She scooped Freddie up and carried her through the house to the waterbed. She undid her bra completely, feasted on one teat and then the next. Freddie moaned, ever so softly.

"Is that the best you can do, sweetie? I bet you can moan better than that." She ran her teeth over her breasts and licked and sucked with more gusto. Freddie whimpered. "Now we're getting somewhere."

Stephanie, growing extremely warm, shucked the sundress. When Freddie tugged on her shorts, Stephanie smacked her hand away. "No. I've had my eye on these all day."

She reached down and stuck her hand up one leg of the shorts.

Freddie was holding her breath. She ran her fingers through the stickiness, and Freddie groaned. "Please," she begged.

"My, my, are we anxious?" Together, Freddie and Stephanie removed the shorts. Both naked, they rolled around breast to breast kissing and feeling each other. "Shit. Pepper."

Now what? The dog had relieved herself. She recalled seeing some biscuits in a bowl.

Stephanie shot out of bed and ran out on the lanai in her birthday suit. She proceeded to herd Pepper back in, wipe off her feet and close the screen door. Freddie stood in the doorway to the living area and watched this big passionate woman gently wipe off the dog and secure their den. A lump formed in her throat. It was mind-numbing that although she'd only known this woman for hours, her feelings for Stephanie already went beyond raw lust. She was getting in over her head at an astounding pace.

Stephanie was now filling a water bowl in the kitchen and washing her hands. The whole house opened off the living area and Freddie could see into every room. The warm thoughts that flooded over her as she watched Stephanie go through her various little chores caused her mind to wander and threw her off guard. She practically fell over when Stephanie approached and looped her arm around her naked waist. Helping her regain her balance, Stephanie led her back to bed.

"Have you wiped the iguana's butt and fed the Venus fly trap?" Freddie teased.

With a mere wisp of the local dialect, Stephanie retorted, "That's what we're about to do here, yeah?" Not giving Freddie a chance for a witty reply, Stephanie placed a cool hand between her legs. "So much for the foreplay, kewpie doll."

Freddie was surprised at both the name and the sensation. She could feel the ball of Stephanie's thumb pressing against her and another finger working its way inside of her. At that moment, she was sure that all the jokes about going blind from illicit sex were based on fact. Her vision was becoming blurred. She shut her eyes and rocked back and forth and side to side with each plunging sensation. Stephanie tweaked a nipple with her free hand and ran her leg down the length of Freddie's leg. Freddie forced herself up and found Stephanie's mouth pulling her tongue into her own mouth. When the passion became too intense, she lowered herself back onto the bed and rode out the waves.

She had never been particularly shy during sex, but she sounded like a banshee to herself as she exploded in orgasm. Egging her on, playing her like a stringed instrument and pushing her even further over the edge, Stephanie was shouting, "Yes. Come on baby. Yes. Get it all out. Yes!"

Her body still quaking, Freddie began to laugh and then to cry.

"Are you okay?" Stephanie asked her, stroking hair, damp with perspiration, off her forehead.

"I don't think I've ever been better."

"You sounded terrific."

"I just feel...emotional," she said with a slight sob.

"That's okay. You can cry if you want. I feel very powerful reducing the great teacher to tears."

"You're bad!" Freddie hoisted herself up so she could look at Stephanie's face.

"How bad am I?" Stephanie countered.

"Very bad."

Stephanie cleared her throat. "What do you do to bad girls, Teach? Gonna spank me?"

"Oooh..." Freddie groaned. "Roll over!" There they were, exactly as she had remembered them from the dream. Those alabaster cheeks. She cupped them in her hand and gave each side a little tap. "I'm having déjà vu."

"Do you really spank students? I thought there were laws... Hey! I thought it was the student who was supposed to kiss the teacher's ass!" Freddie placed feathery kisses up one buttock and down the other. She kissed Stephanie's hips and trailed her tongue behind her knees. Stephanie twitched and giggled.

Hmm...a ticklish spot. She doubled back and licked and kissed her way up her back. She straddled Stephanie and kissed her shoulders, both sides of her neck, and her ear lobes. She brushed one hand against the side of a breast and reached beneath to cup it in her hand. The malleability of the waterbed assisted her in her exploration. She climbed off of Stephanie's back and reassessed her strategy. "Turn on your side."

"You're enjoying being in charge entirely too much."

"I said turn on your side...or suffer the consequences." She began a tickle attack behind one knee. Stephanie squealed and withdrew her leg, turning on her side.

Freddie lay down and faced her again. "Don't mess with me. I usually get what I want."

"Uhmm."

Freddie trailed her fingers around Stephanie's nipples. They were instantly hard. She put her mouth over them and tasted them in succession. Stephanie cooed in appreciation. Choosing the left breast, she sank her teeth into the areola as she swirled her tongue around the nipple. Stephanie responded with a loud cartoon character gulp. Lying on her side was almost too much work. Stephanie flopped over on her back.

"Un-uh. You didn't say, 'Teacher, may I?'" She held Stephanie's face in her hands. "I'll let it pass with a tongue lashing." She buried her tongue in Stephanie's mouth and they did a slow lingual tango.

Freddie finally let her up for a bit of air. *If this is the appetizer, I may die before the main course.* Stephanie opened her mouth to direct, but Freddie kissed her again and wedged one knee between Stephanie's legs. Stephanie ground against Freddie's knee, gritted her teeth, and groaned. Freddie moved down her body and parted her folds with one hand and stroked her with the other. Stephanie fingered her own nipples.

"Ooh, that's good. That's so-o good."

"I'm glad."

Stephanie's hips set the rhythm and Freddie stroked her. She shifted her position and managed to penetrate her with her thumb. Stephanie sighed and her hips gyrated even faster. Freddie was starting to feel a numbing tingle in her hands when Stephanie shattered into a climax. She clamped down on Freddie's hand and pleaded, "Don't move."

Freddie sat for several seconds, feeling the tiny aftershocks of Stephanie's orgasm. She glanced down at her hand, still between Stephanie's legs. She felt so good, so high, so pleased at the other woman's pleasure. If this sweet prize, quivering in her hands, was her payback for her husband screwing his secretary, she didn't mind being a living cliché. Could it be that life was one cliché after another? She was as out of the closet as a person could get, and her hand was definitely in the cookie jar.

A Few Hours Later

FREDDIE STOOD OVER STEPHANIE, WATCHING her sleep. Stephanie had rolled onto her stomach, and the moonlight danced along her prone figure. She stirred.

"Stephanie?"

"Huh. Oh, I guess I fell asleep." She sniffed. "Geez, you must be starving. I have some eggs and stuff. I hope you helped yourself."

"Come on. I made us something to eat."

Stephanie hoisted herself off the waterbed and became instantly self-conscious. She reached for a robe. Freddie appeared to be wearing some old red T-shirt of Stephanie's. "Smells good."

"I just poked around and helped myself in the kitchen. Hope you don't mind."

The table was set with the good plates, which hadn't been out in months, and the real crystal goblets. There were candles lit. Freddie dished out rice from the rice cooker. One dish seemed to be stir-fried asparagus and mushrooms. The other was some type of egg foo young. Freddie pulled the tab on a beer and divided it between the two glasses.

It was almost eerie eating a real meal on real plates in this house. Since Jill's departure, Stephanie had subsisted on macaroni and cheese that she scooped up with potato chips. Stephanie's cooking was legendary, but taking the trouble to cook just for herself was scarcely a possibility.

"This is good. I didn't know anyone from the Mainland knew how to use a rice cooker."

"I lived in Japan for three years." Conversation stopper. The words hung in the air, punctuating the niggling self-doubts and the hard reality that they didn't know very much about each other.

Stephanie pushed her plate away. She stopped and thought. Rubbing the leftover sand out of her eyes, she turned toward Freddie. "Look," she began, her eyes involuntarily shifting to Freddie's chest. A wave of uncontrollable laughter racked her body. Tears began streaming down her face, she was laughing so hard.

"What?" Freddie asked in a panic. "Have I got egg on my face? Oh. I took this shirt off the hook in the bathroom. Oh, no. Sorry...I must have gotten some sauce on it when I was cooking. I can wash it. I know it would come out."

Stephanie started coughing and choking from the laughter. She bit the inside of her cheek to stop herself. The Bambi-in-the-headlights expression on Freddie's face was heart-wrenching. "What I was going to say was, I want to know every detail, no matter how tiny, of your life before you got that craving for Mexican food. But first, I really want you come over here." She grabbed Freddie's hand and walked her over to a full-length mirror in the hall next to the bathroom. "Don't worry about the food spot, the shirt was another gift from Jill. You keep stumbling across them. Just take a look at it."

"What? I know it's some diving thing. I saw the international symbol on it..."

Stephanie stood behind her with her arms around Freddie's neck. She let one finger loose and traced the letters on the shirt. Freddie looked in the mirror. It read: "Professional Muff Dive Instructor." The shirt was a bit long on Freddie. The bottom of it, which had a head buried between a woman's legs, hit Freddie in just the right spot. Freddie turned redder than the T-shirt, averted her eyes from the mirror, and tried to squirm away.

Stephanie tightened her grip. "Oh, come on. I thought you had such a great sense of humor."

"Right. In the ten hours you've known me, I've been a barrel of monkeys. Usually, I'm as serious as a heart attack."

The words stung. Yes, it had not even been a full half-day.

"Are we having our first fight?" Stephanie twirled her around and looked deeply into her eyes. Freddie's legs buckled and Stephanie drew her close to her. "I was just playing. You can trust me."

"I have little choice. You've kidnapped me and taken me up to your lair in the mountains. And, based on results, I may never walk straight again."

"Oh, honey. I hope you never do anything 'straight' again!" Freddie actually managed a chuckle at that one. Stephanie led her over to the sofa and they sat down. Pepper jumped up on the sofa between them and snuggled in. "Thanks, Pep, we need someone to keep us off each other for five seconds."

"I'm afraid," Freddie murmured.

"Of what?"

"Of everything. Of this, of us. It's all been so easy. I'm worried that it's too easy. You know your way around...these things much better than I do."

Stephanie understood what she meant, but it still felt insulting. Stephanie turned to look into her eyes. She couldn't quite read the expression. She paused for a long time.

When she found the words she began, "Didn't you think it might be a little different with a woman? More honest, closer to the bone? Maybe it's so easy because we were looking for the same thing."

"I'm not sure I did think, I just...acted."

"When we were exchanging relationship histories, I could tell we had a lot in common. In the past, we've both missed obvious signs. I know that we've been together for mere hours, but I can't think of a goddamn thing that's missing." She softened her voice. "Can you?"

"No."

That was more like it. "Freddie, just because I'm the one who's been with women before doesn't mean that I have ever felt the way I have today. I don't have anything to compare this with. I've had a handful of relationships and I barely even kissed them on the first date, let alone..."

"I was thinking that since we came back here, it was like the second date."

"Don't you know the lesbian stereotype?"

"No."

"The second date is when you move in together. Now think about that if you want something to scare the hell out of you."

"I have no doubts about you. My doubts are about me. I know that we don't know each other, but I feel like I've known you forever. Actually, I think I had a dream about you after I saw you that first night in the restaurant."

Stephanie sat up straight. "This ought to be good."

"It was just a piece of a dream, actually. I had my hands on your...bare butt. It was a real dream thing where I could be in different places at once. My hands were wrapped around your rear end, yet I could see it. It had the same cast that your bottom has in the moonlight on your waterbed."

Stephanie gasped for air. "You're doing it to me again. I may have to kick the dog off the couch and take you right here." Stephanie moved in closer and kissed Freddie. Pepper complained at being crushed between their hips.

"There's more."

"I'm all ears. Well, maybe not."

"I went to the gallery and I saw your fish photos. There was the surgeon fish with the gold ring around its eyes—the *kole*."

"Sure. The gold-ringed surgeon fish."

"Well, in my mind, I was calling you *kole* because of the gold flecks in your eyes. And then I'm in this shop and I hear these local people talking and I figure out that *okole* means..."

"Okay. I see where this is going. Most people wait until they know me to call me an asshole."

"I thought it meant more like bottom..."

"I think it means both, actually." She stroked Freddie's hair. "Kewpie doll..."

"Yeah... Where did *that* come from?"

"That's what I called you in my mind after seeing you in the restaurant. k.d. All small letters in my mind, like k.d. lang."

"I...I was afraid that I had imagined the stuff in the restaurant, until I saw you in the gallery again, Stephanie."

"I was trying not to stare, but you winked at me."

"What? No, I didn't."

"Yes, you did. You winked at me."

"It must have been a twitch. I was just out of control."

"I'll buy that. Actually, I had a dream too. I mean, I think it was about you. It was hard to tell. I was..." She stopped.

"What? Tell me. I told you!"

"I was certifying you for the T-shirt you're wearing."

Freddie blushed and turned away. Stephanie picked up Pepper, placed her on the floor, and moved in closer to Freddie. Freddie was still looking away and had her hands folded across her chest, covering up the incriminating lettering. Stephanie nuzzled her neck and reached under the long shirt, prying Freddie's arms from covering her chest. She ran her nails along Freddie's belly and up her stomach. "You know, this is a hell of a time to decide you're shy." She traced one of Freddie's nipples with her fingers. Immediate reaction. "Ooh, not shy there." Stephanie reached for the other one. "Hmm, this one isn't shy, either."

"Traitors!" Freddie declared.

Freddie gazed deeply into Stephanie's eyes. "What's happening to me?"

"Whatever it is, I think it's contagious." Stephanie lowered her lips onto Freddie's. She nibbled her lips and probed with her tongue. Freddie teased back with her own tongue and reached up to run her fingers through Stephanie's brunette mane.

Freddie was feeling her excitement build and working up the nerve to reach for Stephanie when the other woman disengaged abruptly. Freddie swallowed a lump of disappointment. What did the dog need this time?

Stephanie began clearing the table and wrapping up their barely eaten dinner. "Let me get this stuff cleaned up," she offered by way of explanation. Freddie got up to help and Stephanie motioned her away. "Sit down and relax. You've done plenty—making real food out of the meager offerings in my kitchen. Besides, I think you should save your strength. I have plans!"

# Plans B and A

THE TILED SHOWER STALL WAS cozy for two, but nobody was complaining. Stephanie rubbed the soft bar between her hands to create billows of foam. She reached around Freddie and lathered the soap into her breasts in large counter-clockwise circles. Freddie moaned her approval.

They lathered each other repeatedly, caressing as they went. Freddie scrubbed Stephanie's back with a sponge, pushing her gently against the tiled wall of the shower. The cool tile tantalized her nipples. Freddie's body blocked most of the spray of the shower as she moved her abdomen against Stephanie's backside. She ran the sponge down one of Stephanie's hips and gently reached between her legs with the other hand.

"I don't think I can stand up much longer," Stephanie confessed. Freddie peeled herself off of Stephanie. Stephanie ducked into the spray for one last rinse and turned off the water. She pulled a huge terry cloth bath sheet over her front and pressed Freddie to her as they edged out of the shower. Stephanie opened the bathroom door to get some fresh air, and they slowly tangoed into the hallway. It was unclear who was drying whom and what was pressing against what as they slid down against the wall and began to roll around on the floor.

Stephanie had intended to get them back to the bedroom, but they didn't make it that far. In the hallway, working hard not to bang her head against the door, Stephanie Amalfi's tongue lapped over and over again at her swollen clitoris, and Freddie Shapiro's eyes rolled back in her head as she experienced the most intense orgasm of her life. She shrieked so long that Pepper began to bark at the racket. When she was calm enough to speak again, her throat was raw.

"Oh, my god."

"Was that okay? I graduated with highest honors from my diving class."

"Ah…"

Stephanie helped her to her feet and led her to the bed. They lay pressed together in a sweet embrace. Stephanie caressed Freddie's back. Freddie nibbled at her neck.

Stephanie was beginning to drift off when Freddie surprised her. "I think I'm ready for an intro dive," she whispered hoarsely. She was contemplating a rain check when Freddie teased her sleepy nipples awake. Freddie continued down her body trailing her tongue across her belly. Stephanie placed a pillow under her own hips and used both her hands to allow Freddie easy access. Once again, Freddie was a quick study.

When her breathing finally returned to normal, Stephanie said, "Oh, honey, you can keep that T-shirt. You earned it."

Freddie maneuvered herself up on the waterbed amid slight ripples. She snuggled against Stephanie and kissed her. Stephanie's eyes grew heavy. Sleep was about to claim her again.

"When did you know?" Freddie asked.

Her eyes fluttered open. The intonation and the weight of the words hit Stephanie with force.

"You want to know when I knew I was a dyke?"

"Yes."

Stephanie blinked herself awake. "I told you about the little dalliance with my college roommate, but initially I was willing to think of that as a one-time thing. I guess when I really figured it out was in my early twenties. I'd just broken up with some guy and I met a woman at a party. I liked her instantly. She had a great sense of humor and she made me feel good. I felt a real connection. We met for coffee a few times. I found myself thinking about her other times and feeling…tingly." Stephanie felt Freddie's hand begin stroking her back.

"And?"

Stephanie yawned. "A few days later, we had a drink at her house. We were supposed to go to the movies, but we never got there. We were sitting on the sofa and our hands brushed. It was electric. She touched my face and kissed me. I felt like a character in a fairy tale. She'd awakened something in me. That was when I knew."

They were both quiet. Within seconds, Stephanie was out like a light again. Before sleep overcame her, Freddie could hear Stephanie's voice in her mind: "*She'd awakened something in me.*"

Very Early the Next Morning

WITH THOUSANDS OF YEARS OF guilt woven into the fabric of her genetic background, Freddie always reasoned that she came by such feelings honestly. She had been awake for half an hour and the clock said 4:56. Sitting on the sofa, she covered her face with her hands. She was reeling from the shock of the dramatic turn her life had taken in the past 24 hours.

She had spent hours and hours beneath the sheets, on sofas, and even on the floor with a woman. Not a man, a woman. She didn't know the woman's favorite color or middle name, but she knew every freckle, hair, and ticklish spot on her body.

Thinking back to the intense sexual excitement gave her chills and caused actual physical convulsions, but her mind was starting to judge and referee. Something had awakened in her to be sure, but maybe it needed to go back to sleep. She felt as if her conscience had missed the ride to Stephanie's and had walked over to rejoin her at 4:00 a.m. Fornicator's remorse was relatively incurable—at least with buyer's remorse, you could return the item and try to get your money back.

Why hadn't she stopped when Stephanie had to go home to her dog? That was her last opportunity—maybe even an attempt at divine intervention; after all, dog spelled backwards was... Now she really was being silly. She could think of it as an experiment, a very satisfying experiment that she had to see through. You can't just pour the chemicals into separate beakers to find out how they react, you have to mix them together. She would thank Stephanie for a lovely evening and they'd each remember the time together fondly.

A light went on behind her. Stephanie paled when she saw the grave look on Freddie's face. She sat down in a chair across from her and waited.

Freddie made a brief attempt at levity. "Don't you know the joke? How many Jewish mothers does it take to change a light bulb?" She didn't wait for an answer. "It's okay, I'd rather sit in the dark."

Stephanie tried to laugh, but she was overcome with panic. Recovering slightly, she forced a grin. "I tried to fuck your brains out, but I obviously missed a spot. Otherwise, you wouldn't be out here at this ungodly hour *thinking!*"

Freddie started to cry.

"I'm sorry, " Stephanie said automatically. "Is it my lousy sense of humor? The F-word? I can clean up my act. I promise."

"No, it's not you. You're funny, beautiful, warm, loving…"

"Well, if you're going to be insulting…"

"And I don't deserve you."

The panic was back, causing a stabbing pain in Stephanie's head. This couldn't be over. Not this quickly. "I'm usually quite non-violent, but if you say 'Let's just be friends,' I may have to slap you."

Freddie resumed her crying jag.

Stephanie slumped further down in the chair. The no dyke-virgin rule had been a really good one. She was an imbecile to forgo it. Forget that it was the best sex she had ever had. Forget that absolutely everything felt right with this woman. They were in different places in their life. She had dealt with these issues almost half a lifetime ago. She didn't even know how old Freddie was, although she assumed they were close in age.

"Please, Freddie. Talk to me." The silence continued with Freddie sniffling softly. "I don't want you to be miserable. Believe it or not, I *do* know what you are going through. And what you do next, naturally, is up to you. You can turn around and pretend that what happened between us didn't. Maybe you'll be the exception to the rule, but in my experience, coming out of the closet is a one-way journey. It's the original can of worms—once you're out, it's virtually impossible to get yourself back in. Of course, if you felt even a quarter of what I did last night, I don't know why you'd want to turn away from this."

Freddie found a tissue and blew her nose loudly. "I'm so confused." The tear-induced congestion gave her voice an even huskier quality. "It was so easy yesterday. When we were caressing and…" She swallowed hard and continued, "...making love, everything was so easy. All I wanted to do was touch you, but when I had a little time to think about it, I wasn't sure who I was. I mean before yesterday I was a...I don't know..."

"An out-of-practice heterosexual?" Stephanie offered.

"And then, before I knew it, I was a..." she faltered once again.

"An insatiable lesbian?"

"You say you aren't enjoying my pain, but you seem to be getting off on this!"

"I'm playing with you, yes. Not to turn the screw, so to speak, but to cajole you into not taking yourself so seriously." Stephanie paused and took a deep breath. "There is something that works really well with this kind of confusion."

"What's that?"

"Time."

Freddie smiled at her. She was exhausted, but convinced that Stephanie really did understand how she was feeling. They decided that Freddie should get back to the hotel and get some more sleep. Freddie would call Stephanie after she had had some time to sort out her feelings.

Stephanie pulled up in front of the King Kamehameha hotel. It was still very early and there were no bell captains or any other sign of life. She wanted to kiss Freddie full on the lips and tell her that every minute she spent away from these mutual sensations would be a minute of her life wasted, but instead she took Freddie's delicate hand and kissed the knuckles gently. She finally said, "If we were following my conscience and my heart, I wouldn't let you get five feet away, but we're not. I hope to hear from you soon, kewpie doll. I hope you will get to a place where you can accept yourself. When that happens, we can make love until we're weak in the knees and you'll sleep in, like a normal person."

"Forgive me for being a pain in the *okole*, my sweet *kole*. I think you're right about 'time.' I just need a little time to get my mind and body back into synch." They smiled at one another and Freddie got out of the car.

Stephanie pulled out of the hotel driveway and drove up to one of the shopping center parking lots. It was early and there were no cars there. She turned off the motor and sobbed uncontrollably for the next half hour.

Late Afternoon

As the day wore on, Stephanie found herself alternating between sadness and anger. She could still smell Freddie in the air, on her skin. She procrastinated for hours before she took another shower.

She replayed the day before with alternative endings. *If only she had led me on, even for a day.* It would have been great to wander around with the euphoria that accompanies a new relationship. *Why couldn't I have had one day of walking with my feet not quite touching the ground?*

Or, if she had called a cab and sneaked out in the middle of the night, no guilt, no tears, just a torrid affair with nobody looking back. But no, she wounded me. And what did I do? I clutched my bleeding heart and empathized. I was the understanding one. What was I thinking?

Just before noon, she was sitting on the lanai and she caught sight of three baby wild turkeys wobbling across the cane grass in the distance. She was telling Freddie about them in her mind. She bit her lip to stop from crying once again. Anger was better, she reasoned; it pushed away the hurt.

Her face felt hot and her throat burned. *That stupid little cunt tease. Okay, that wasn't really fair, she put out and I didn't even have to buy a nice dinner. It only cost me a few eggs—well, that, and all of my self-respect and integrity. I managed to get to the ripe old age of forty-one avoiding casual sex. Why have I broken all the rules now? I knew better.*

Maybe she didn't like our time together as much as I thought. Yeah, right. Remembering the sweet abandon in Freddie, the way she had shuddered and convulsed against her mouth as they made love, caused Stephanie's stomach to tighten and the sadness to return.

She felt sleepy. She had made vague plans to take pictures of a neighbor's garden that week. She had tentatively slated the shoot for late that afternoon, but the thought of leaving the house was too overwhelming. She couldn't face the world. It was 4:00 p.m. She still clung to the faint hope that Freddie would call and apologize for freaking out that morning, so she didn't want to be more than three feet from the telephone. Why had she been so damn understanding? Think about everything. Take your time. That was a crock. Why hadn't she painted a beautiful picture of the gay divorcée and her adoring lesbian lover? *I could make you very happy, if you'd just give me a chance,* she said to Freddie over and over in her mind.

Realizing how seriously she wanted to make Freddie happy was an epiphany. She wasn't completely beyond feeling sorry for herself, but what she felt for Freddie was a lot more than lasciviousness. She needed to stop beating herself up; this wasn't about casual sex. Fate had brought them together. Freddie hadn't hesitated even for a moment around her, despite her annoying afterthoughts. This had to be going on for Freddie, as well. Both of them had known, with absolute certainty, that they were meant to be together. The issue was whether they were meant to be together for 18 hours or forever and ever. Stephanie realized she wanted the latter.

Somewhere deep down, she had always hoped to feel the passion that she had felt in the past day. Somehow, her body had realized how special this relationship was before her mind caught up. She had loved other women, but she was in love with Freddie Shapiro. So much for the good news. The bad news was, she may never get the chance to tell her.

She hadn't felt this with any of her former lovers. That explained why she had not followed Jill back to New York. The relationship had not been worth fighting for. She'd been angry and hurt before, but this felt like her soul had been excised, leaving her to live in an empty shell of a body. The only way to be whole again was to map out a plan of attack and fight for Freddie. A brief flash of her carrying Freddie out of a science class like the factory scene in *An Officer and a Gentleman*, complete with background music, caused her to chuckle in spite of herself. If she went down, it would be screaming and kicking—no should'ves, would'ves, could'ves to haunt her. But, if she succeeded...

She curled up on the couch in a fetal position. Depression, followed by thinking about putting up a good fight, had taken all the energy out of Stephanie's body. She fell into a deep sleep. She dreamed of making love with Freddie on a boat in the middle of the ocean.

Sunset

FREDDIE HAD BEEN TALKING NON-STOP for more than five minutes. She had glossed over a few of the juicier details, but she had given her cousin the gist of the past evening's activities.

"Could you repeat that? I'm not sure I caught it all," Sue teased.

"I'd bet my next royalty check that you heard every damn word," Freddie countered. "I'm a wreck. Believe it or not, I can't eat. I can't work. I can't even stand looking at the ocean or listening to that everybody-get-happy Hawaiian music over the hotel speakers. I just keep going over and over it in my mind. I was an animal. I had wild sex with someone I had known for mere hours. I just can't believe it. I was there, I did it, but I can't believe it."

"There are far worse things than making love to someone, Freddie."

"True, I guess."

"Geez. It is a pretty amazing story."

"Yeah."

"You'll have to lose the wallflower act, though, you sly dog. I think of myself as somebody who's been around the block, but lord. More than once, and on the floor on the first date. Impressive. I guess it's not out of character; you've always been very thorough. I've never known you to do anything halfway."

"Nope, not me. 'All the way Freddie.' I guess I'm just a slut. I've never done anything like this before. I can't even look in the mirror." Her voice trickled to a choked monotone.

Sue was horrified. Just when she thought the conversation was taking a lighter turn, her cousin was losing it. It sounded as if Freddie was on the verge of crying. "It's okay, Freddie. I was just joking around. You have needs. You're entitled to walk on the wild side for once in your life. Not every relationship is by the book. Would you be this distraught if you went to bed with some guy you met in a bar?"

"Probably. I guess I would. I don't know. Oh, Susie, I'm just so confused. I hate myself. I don't want to be like this." The tears burst through. Freddie made a series of choking noises and then appeared to regain her composure.

"Like what? A homophobe or a dyke?"

"Do you really think I'm a homophobe?" she gasped.

"It doesn't matter what I think. We're talking about what you think."

"I think I'm low and cowardly. I never felt as exposed as I did with her. It was the most open, most honest experience I ever had and then I walked away with my tail between my legs. She probably thinks I'm a homophobe, too."

"Let's do this step by step. For the moment, you need to stop worrying about what she does or doesn't think and figure out what you can do to put yourself back together."

"It's weird being here. It's a gorgeous place but I'm so locked into the noise in my head that I can't seem to cancel stuff out and enjoy this. I've even thought about going back to L.A. to sort things out."

"Is that what you need?"

"I need to have something familiar around me—anything."

"How about some*one*?"

"What?"

"I just wrapped up a big case this morning and I was thinking of taking five days off, maybe a week. I wanted to take Nicki to Aruba for a romantic vacation, but there's no way she could get away now. She's tied up with this big project and getting home after 10:00. We end up chatting over a pizza for half an hour and she's ready to go to sleep."

"You'd be willing to come all the way over here?"

"I'm taking this time off, come hell or high water. I need a break. If the choice is between eating junk food and watching soap operas or drinking mai tais and watching Hawaiian sunsets...well, call me a fool, but I vote for Hawaii."

"That would be great, that would be..." Freddie stopped to think for a minute. It would be wonderful to spend time with Sue, and Sue would understand her better than anyone. They'd always been close and Sue was an expert in the field of lesbian love. On the other hand, what if she came to the conclusion that she had had her first and last gay encounter? Would Sue take it personally?

"You're so subtle. I can practically hear the gears in your brain clicking on my end. I don't care if you come out or shove yourself back in. I'll listen, I won't judge you, and I'll keep you from jumping off a tall building."

"They don't have any tall buildings here."

"Good. One less job for me; I'm supposed to be on vacation!"

Freddie sat on her bed shaking her head. Sue was something else. It would be so nice to see her. She got up and opened the curtains. Once again, it was almost sunset in Kona. She thought about the view from Stephanie's and blew out a breath. *Sweet Stephanie.* God, she didn't want to hurt her. She didn't think she could be around her until she handled some of her issues. *Does she really understand?* The ringing phone made her jump, jarring her out of a ponderous haze.

"I get in at 5:06 tomorrow evening on Aloha Airlines. How will I recognize you? It's been months."

"I'll wear one of my bright red streetwalker outfits. I've been attracting a lot of attention lately, you know."

"I heard something like that."

Shortly after she hung up the phone, Freddie got out her computer and set herself up to get online. She hadn't checked her mail in a couple of days and it had accumulated. There was a note from her editor repeating most of what they'd clarified over the phone about the photo budget. Would Stephanie still want the job if they parted ways? She was suddenly filled with a sadness that she could not quite explain.

Freddie spent the next few hours surfing for the definitive answer to the gay gene question. She shared fifty percent of Sue's gene pool; did that explain anything? She found less research and more radical reactionary rhetoric than she had anticipated. When she switched her search words to "latent homosexuality," the majority of the hits centered on barbs at evil conservatives. When she added the word "lesbian," the two-bit "adult" sites multiplied furiously. The word "lesbian" itself was the richest content area she pinpointed; it drew seven figures out in cyberspace.

While she assigned potential comfort to delving into the worlds of science and technology on this issue, she quickly realized that all the scientific support in the world was not going to clear the path for her. Her answers would need to come from the inside. "That little exercise was quite illogical, Captain," she told herself in her best Mr. Spock imitation. She had accomplished little else than killing several hours.

She'd also managed to successfully ignore another romantic Kona sunset. It was dark outside already. *Is it too early to go to bed?* Lack of sleep was gnawing at her. Giving into it, she turned off the computer and crawled under the covers.

Overboard

THE SUN WAS SETTING AND *they were all alone a few miles from shore.* *Freddie was naked except for a sailing cap. They had been making slow, passionate love. Stephanie had her faced buried between Freddie's legs. Freddie pressed for more urgency. She moaned and howled. She called out, "Don't stop!" over and over again.*

Stephanie lifted her head and let her fingers take over, quickening her pace. She repeated the same lines over and over to Freddie, "Don't worry, baby, I won't stop. Come on, sweetie. That's it." At last, Freddie came in sharp thrusts, screaming at the top of her lungs.

They sat up and stared into one another's eyes. "I want you," Freddie said in a deep, husky voice. "Come here."

As Stephanie moved to be closer to Freddie, Freddie pulled herself over the side and started to swim to shore. "It's too far, Freddie! You can't go back. It's close to sunset. There may be sharks. Come back, Freddie. Don't do this!"

Stephanie awoke feeling miserable and spent. Her nap had been anything but restful. She'd barely eaten all day, and that combined with the emotional turmoil had caused a bad case of heartburn. She found a bottle of antacids and chewed two. She took Pepper through her evening rituals and even managed to play "go get it" for a few minutes. Pepper, sensing that her owner was not all there, cut the game short and crawled under a chair.

Stephanie picked up the phone and put it down several times. Pepper snorted. *Disapproving or disturbed?* She finally picked it up again and dialed.

"Hi, Leilani. It's Stephanie Amalfi."

"Hi. How are you?"

"Oh, fine." *Big lie.* "And you?"

"Good."

"I wanted to order an Aloha basket. Would you still be able to get one out today? I know it's late."

"I could make it up, but FedEx is closed already."

"No, no. I want to send it to someone who is staying at the King Kam."

"The King Kam? No problem. I need to go *makai** to do some grocery shopping. I could drop it off about 7:30."

"Wonderful."

They decided on salted macadamia nuts, chocolate-covered macadamia nuts, coffee candy, and two pounds of ground pure Kona coffee. Draped around the handle of the basket would be a fresh plumeria lei and a card. Stephanie gave her the name, room number and the message. Leilani wrote the message out and signed as her proxy.

"I'm thinking of you.

Love,

Steph."

Arranging for the gift had an amazingly calming effect on Stephanie. She read the newspaper and then watched TV for a few hours. At 9:15, she sat down with a stack of bills and wrote checks. She took inventory and made several shopping lists. She needed film and batteries for work. She was also low on food for both herself and Pepper. She jumped when the phone rang. As she picked it up, she could feel her heart hammering in her chest.

"Stephanie, hi. It's Allison. Sorry to call so late. I'm still at work."

Allison Murray was the editor of a guidebook for which Stephanie had shot pictures. She was the first lesbian with whom Stephanie had had any professional dealings in Hawaii. "How're you doing? How's the book coming?"

"I think we are finally at the last proof stage."

"Great."

"Are you busy tomorrow?"

"Why?"

"I really need you to check that all the photos look right and have been cropped correctly. I want you to come over to Honolulu. We'll pay, of course. We'll even spring for lunch."

She'd better find a greater incentive than lunch. The last time a client had offered to buy lunch, it had led to major trouble. If Freddie was holed up in her hotel room, she'd had two hours since the basket arrived to call.

"You still there, Stephanie?"

"Yeah, sorry. When would you need me there?"

"I tentatively have you booked on the 7:05 Aloha flight here and the one that gets back at 5:06. You and Jill could still go out to dinner."

Stephanie cleared her throat. "There isn't a 'me and Jill' anymore."

"Sorry. I can be such a clod."

"It's okay. It's not like we took out an ad in the community or anything."

"You know, there's a hot local woman I know in Kona. She broke up with her lover last year and she's been really lonely."

"Look, it's an incredibly long story, but I'm kind of involved with someone else already. If we get through with the proofs early and I'm not feeling like total garbage, I'll tell you about it tomorrow."

"Cool. You need to be at the ticket counter by 6:30. Tell them it's a 'Will Call' and the confirmation is: 2876GH2."

"Hang on. This pen isn't writing."

After double-checking the confirmation number and signing off, Stephanie sank down into a chair. She looked at the clock. It was five minutes to ten. "I guess she isn't going to call us, Pep. She could have, you know. We pay the stupid fee for 'call-us interrupt-us' just for times like this." Pepper cocked her ears, trying to discern whether or not, "snack," "walk," "out," or "bed," her four favorite words, had been used.

Stephanie opened the lanai and let Pepper run around the yard for a few minutes. She whistled and Pepper came back in. "Sorry, Pep, I need to go get us some food and stuff." At the very least, the grocery shopping had to be taken care of before the early morning trip.

Why hadn't she called? Maybe two pounds of coffee was going overboard; would toffee chews have been the key to her heart? She had hoped for an immediate reaction. Stephanie started Honda-Honey and applied very little gas to coast down the hill into town.

makai = toward the ocean

Phone Tag

FREDDIE WOKE UP AT 10:15, groggy from the nap. She opened her eyes for a second and then closed them. *So much for sleeping through the night!* She had dreamed about Stephanie again, this time from the front. She remembered one part of the dream clearly. She was sucking on Stephanie's breasts. She resurrected the scene in her head and saw the whole thing again along with a silly little conversation.

"Has anyone ever told you that your…" What word would describe them? Breasts sounded too clinical. "…That your knockers are delicious?"

"My knockers? Hmm. Maybe. I don't kiss and tell."

"They have slightly different flavors."

"Really? I hope one is macadamia nut and the other Kona coffee. I want you to have the full local experience."

She opened her eyes. The light on her telephone was flashing. Had she slept through a phone call? She called the front desk. They had a package for her. Someone from the bell desk would bring it up shortly. A package? Probably Steve trying to suck up.

She gave the guy a dollar and took the huge basket from him. Reading the card, she began to shake. Okay, it was hard to go very far in Kona without tripping over some macadamia nuts or Kona coffee, but how synchronistic. She had dreamed about discussing them with Stephanie and here they were in a basket from her. Maybe Stephanie was some kind of sorceress.

Her fingers were still trembling as she dialed the number on Stephanie's card. It rang five times. Just as she was about to hang up, an answering machine kicked in. "Hi, this is Steph. Leave a message. Mahalo."

"Stephanie, it's Freddie. The basket…it's beautiful." She paused ever so briefly and continued more softly. "Just like you. I know it isn't fair to you. It's as if all of my feelings for you were in some kind of emotional attic or something. I need a little bit more time to sweep out all the cobwebs. Don't give up on me yet, Kole!" She tried to keep the sob out of her voice, but it preceded her last words. "Sweet dreams."

Curses, Foiled Again

STEPHANIE SET THE GROCERIES ON the table. The light on the answering machine was flashing frantically. The little man's voice on the IC chip informed her in even tones that she had one message, which came in at 10:47. The tape engaged and she heard Freddie's voice. "Fucking A," she cursed in a booming voice, causing Pepper to turn back her ears in fear.

Stephanie switched ears, took a deep breath, and gave a slightly edited, yet nevertheless detailed version of the past day to Wendy. Talking about it was good.

"You agreed to, no, you suggested some down time," the other woman reminded her. "You have to let her work out whatever she's going through. Coming out is like menopause; some women have more trouble with it than others."

"Whatever. It's just that…my timing sucks. I find the woman of my dreams and she's going through all sorts of stuff. I wait for her to call and she calls during the twenty minutes that I'm out shopping for milk and dog food. I was here all day, damn it."

"It's okay, Steph. Stuff happens," Wendy attempted to comfort her.

"That's 'shit happens,' Wendy. I'm way beyond the G-rated version of emotions with this woman. The only thing that outdoes what I've already done with her is what I've thought about doing with her. And you know what else? I actually like her. I just realized today that I never really liked my other lovers. I loved them, but I didn't like them and I wasn't in love with them. I want this woman like I've never wanted anyone in my life."

"Whoa. That was grounded."

"What do you mean?"

"Well, you know how sometimes someone tells you something and you know it's a bunch of manure, okay, bullshit, and they don't sound like they believe it?"

"Yeah…" Stephanie was afraid she wouldn't like where this was going.

"I had the exact opposite reaction to what you said. I could feel it in my gut that you were telling the god's honest truth about all of this."

Not at all what Stephanie was expecting, but disturbing nonetheless. "I'm dead meat."

"That's one way of putting it."

Planes, Pains and Drains

FREDDIE WOKE UP IN A good mood. Chances were high she'd had some erotic dream, but she couldn't remember anything. She looked at the basket and read the note again. She picked up one of the sacks and sniffed the coffee. It smelled heavenly. Unfortunately, there was no coffee maker in the room. She had the lei strung over one side of the mirror above the dresser. The air conditioning in the room had kept it in reasonable shape—there was just a bit of browning staining the edges, a small price to pay for the room being enveloped in the perfume of the plumeria blossoms.

She folded her arms around her and hugged them to her chest. She pondered the theory of the hour. Maybe this forced separation was unnecessary. Was it that she needed to be alone? Not really. If she absolutely had to be alone, she wouldn't have agreed to Sue's visit. What she needed was to slow down. With Sue in town from that evening, the dynamic would have to change. The non-stop sexual frenzy would have to subside with another person in her life. If there were something to help put the brakes on and she and Stephanie could relax and get to know each other outside of bed, or the floor, maybe that would help resolve some of her conflicts.

She caught herself chewing her fingernails. It was a nasty habit she thought she had kicked years ago. This strong desire to have Stephanie back in her life, was it enough of an answer in and of itself? Or was she playing games? She wanted nothing more than to talk to Stephanie. She picked up the phone.

It was 8:30 a.m. The answering machine got it again. Freddie was a bit surprised that she would be out so early. "Stephanie, it's me again. I need to talk to you. I know I agreed to take some time to think, but I really need to talk to you. Could we get together this afternoon? I'll be at the hotel. Okay. Bye."

She showered and then sat out on her lanai in a long T-shirt reading a book. The phone didn't ring. Once she even walked back into the room, picked up the receiver and checked for a dial tone.

At 11:30, she ordered brunch from room service. Over a turkey sandwich, the doubts began to creep back. Maybe the fact that she kept missing Stephanie meant something. She could just be a two-time loser heterosexual who had a half day affair with a beautiful lesbian. It sounded plausible. She kept getting stuck on the beautiful lesbian part. She remembered the way Stephanie had laughed over the T-shirt. And how she had looked bent over the photographs. And how...

By 12:30, she had scrounged up the nerve to call again. The tollsaver mechanism had kicked in and the answering machine was picking up on the second ring. She hated people who hung up on answering machines, but she wasn't sure what to say the second time, so she joined their ranks.

At 2:00, she decided to go shopping. She would try Stephanie one more time from the road. She tried Stephanie from a pay phone at 4:40. "It's me again," she managed to say. "I need to talk to you." She had really wanted to have a talk with Stephanie before Sue arrived. It was time to head for the airport. Her sunny mood was looking to set with the sun.

She tried to clear her mind. The road to Keahole Airport was easy to drive. Traffic was picking up, but not too bad. The black lava rock looked like moonscape. It was a local custom to bring white coral rocks up from the beach and arrange them in graffiti messages like "Kimo loves Joan" or "In memory of Max." Some of them were just initials. One said, W.S. + S.A. She smiled, seeing her initials in beach rock. When she realized that the other set of initials was Stephanie's, she almost veered off the road.

Was that there before? How would she know; she had only been this far up on the road when she came in from the airport. She wouldn't have seen something on this side of the street before. Was there a guardian angel of lesbians who went around arranging these things? Maybe the gift basket wasn't from Stephanie, after all. She had remembered Stephanie's signature from one of the framed photographs in the gallery. It had been particularly artistic. The one on the card was much simpler and squarer, like the handwriting of an older person.

The knot in her stomach was back. She just wanted to talk to Stephanie again. Stephanie was starting to feel like the best friend she'd never had. She'd already had more conversations with her in her head than in real life. Freddie needed some resolution to their situation. And soon. The biggest problem with riding this long, exciting emotional roller coaster was the butterflies.

🖎　🖎　🖎

Sitting in the waiting area for the plane to Kona, Stephanie thought back on the day's events with a smile. Stephanie had told Allison the basic Freddie story minus some of the angst and some of the truly intimate details. Allison was panting like a dog in heat by the end of the story. If she played her cards right, she'd have the kind of life that other people envied. *Look at so-and-so and what's her name, aren't they sickening.*

She'd made another decision. She was through being such a gentlewoman. She'd go to the friggin' hotel and knock some sense into her. Maybe she'd kiss some sense into her. The method was irrelevant just as long as she got through to her. There was an erotica shop near town. Maybe she could stop off for some flavored massage oil. After one of Stephanie's famous massages, Freddie would be forced to strike the words "tense" and "confused" from her vocabulary.

She shut her eyes and pictured Freddie. The way they had sat in the restaurant with their thighs pressed against one another shamelessly. Strangers on the one hand, old friends, soulmates at another level. Lovers, in perfect rhythm, without any of the usual awkwardness. She opened her eyes and blushed immediately. She had the impression that someone was watching her. The woman across the aisle was alone. She smiled. Stephanie smiled back.

What is this? Old dykes week? She looked like Nancy from Hilo. Maybe this woman was a bit younger. She had lines around her eyes—someone with a demanding job. A Yuppie Dyke. She had jet-black hair, very short and salon-styled. Her eyes were greenish. Short fingernails, casual butch dress—pin-striped long sleeve shirt, sleeves rolled up to the elbows, with straight leg cotton pants covering long legs, dark socks and loafers completing the ensemble. Surely she was on the team.

Stephanie chose an aisle seat in the middle of the plane in the emergency row. The flight attendants blocked out those seats, but Stephanie could easily convince them that she would be strong and capable enough to perform emergency procedures. In exchange for this oath, they let her sit where she would have sufficient legroom. The raven-haired Y.D. from the waiting area was on the other side of the plane in an aisle seat ahead of her.

After the plane took off, as Stephanie saw it, there was barely enough time to drink the juice they throw at you and read the ads in the in-flight magazine before they landed. The Y.D., however, had a notebook PC out and was inputting fast and furiously until they made the shut-it-off-so-it-doesn't-interfere-with-the-equipment announcement. Stephanie was amused and pleased with herself that she could spot the type so accurately.

When it was time to deplane, they made the announcements that they would be opening both the front and rear doors. Stephanie figured she was closer to the rear. Of course, there was a guy who had trouble wedging his bag out of the overhead and refused to get out of the way of those in the aisle. When she finally got out, the Y.D. was several people in front of her. She watched as the woman cleared the entrance. She was greeted by a short woman who draped a lei around her. It seemed that they had their faces together for quite some time. I'm two for two, thought Stephanie; her lover is here to meet her. As she disengaged from the smaller woman, Stephanie was struck with panic. It was Freddie. Freddie looped her arm around the Y.D. and headed toward baggage claim.

Quite certain that Freddie hadn't noticed her, Stephanie changed directions and went to the ladies' room. She washed her face and went to a stall.

"You sure you don't want me to go back and wait for the luggage?" It was Freddie's voice.

"I'm really not worried about someone stealing my jeans," the other woman said in a New York accent as she banged into a stall.

Great, thought Stephanie. *I'm trapped in here listening to Freddie's other lover pee.*

"So, why didn't you just tell her?"

"I wasn't going to leave it on her answering machine. I'm just so relieved you came. I was going nuts. What do you have in this bag anyway? It weighs a ton."

"My computer."

"Your computer? I thought this was a vacation. You promised!"

"Don't worry, I'll be good. I just have a few memos to catch up on."

"That's what you always say!"

The easy intimacy. The casual reference to having something to tell that she couldn't leave on an answering machine. Had anyone ever been strangled in this bathroom before? She bit her tongue to keep from screaming.

She walked halfway to the Hawaiian Air side of the terminal to avoid running into the dynamic duo. She had no luggage for her day trip, so she just went to her car. She started the engine, but sat in the parking lot for a few minutes. *How could you, Freddie? How could you be so low?*

If she hadn't been such a chickenshit, she could have confronted them in the women's room. The adrenaline was pumping so hard, she probably could have taken them both on at once. She wanted to shake Freddie, but she would have been able to wound the yuppie one with words. *Any idea what your sweet thing and I did the other day? Does she call out your name twice, Oh, Yuppie Dyke, Oh, Yuppie Dyke, before she goes over the edge?*

She pulled out of her space suddenly and a car circling the parking lot screeched to a halt to let her out. She waved absently and headed for the booth to pay the parking.

Freddie was just about to curse the absentminded driver who was sitting and sitting in her space and then decided to go when she realized what kind of car it was. "I don't believe this. I think that might be Stephanie. You know, I saw that red Honda on my way in and thought it looked like Stephanie's car. I really think it is. Can you see if there is a decal of a bee on the back left window?"

Sue leaned out the passenger side window, but it didn't help. "Not without breaking my neck."

Stephanie fumbled through her purse to put together the six dollars to pay for the parking. She found a hundred-dollar bill, but that wouldn't do. The driver behind her tooted. "Just a second! Why's everyone always in such a hurry?"

"I know what you mean," the man in the booth agreed. The parking attendant flashed a hang-on-a-second gesture to the car behind hers while she put together a five, two quarters and five dimes.

When Stephanie stuck out her arm with the toll money, Freddie saw the bracelet watch and tooted again. Both the attendant and Stephanie shook their heads and clicked their tongues.

He handed Stephanie a receipt and she thanked him and peeled off. The car behind her tooted again. Freddie was trying to get her head out the window to call after her as she fled the scene.

"She was having trouble finding the change, ma'am. That'll be a dollar fifty. You know, this is Hawaii. You folks are supposed to change over to 'Island time' when you come here."

Thanks for the lecture. "I think she's someone I know. I was trying to get her attention," Freddie snapped back at him. Before he could hand her the receipt, she was out of there. He shook his head and watched the blonde and company in the rental car try to catch up to the brunette in the Honda.

Stephanie pulled onto the highway back to Kailua, almost cutting off a thru-traffic car. She needed to calm down.

〜 〜 〜

"So far, all I know about your friend is that she drives like a maniac and has trouble counting change to pay for parking," Sue teased as Freddie got them out on the highway between speeding cars. "Of course, maybe the two of you were in the same driver's ed class."

"Shut up. Just shut up."

"My, aren't we testy."

"How could I not have seen her? It's a small airport. Maybe she was on a Hawaiian flight."

"What's she look like?"

"Tall. Dark brown hair, medium length. Incredible eyes..."

"Solid build, kinda big?"

"Yeah."

"She was on my flight!"

"Really? Was she wearing a muu muu?"

"No. A Hawaiian shirt and shorts."

Shorts? Freddie tried to imagine Stephanie in shorts. The tugging feeling in the center of her being returned. "Hmm."

"Hmm, indeed. Did I mention that she was checking me out?"

"What?"

"I don't know whether or not she was interested. It was just that 'dyke at eleven o'clock' periscope kind of thing. She looked me over, I'm sure of it."

"And you didn't participate? How'd you remember what she was wearing?"

"I didn't say I didn't participate."

"What does Nicki think of your wandering eyes?"

"I have carte blanche to lust in my heart."

"Lust in your heart? That's cute. I don't think I've heard anyone turn that phrase since the Carter Administration."

"If you're trying to call me old, let me remind you that you're only eighteen months younger. And please slow down. I'd like to make it to my next birthday."

Freddie had maneuvered it so that she was directly behind Stephanie's car. When they got to Palani, Freddie also made the left turn. "I'm sure you must be exhausted, but I need to talk to her now. I don't want to go back to the hotel and wait for the phone to ring like a teenager. And I know she's going home now. She's headed up the hill. Please tell me you don't mind."

"Listen, if you two don't mind being around someone who hasn't showered in seventeen hours, it's fine with me."

Freddie stuck her hand out the window and tried to wave. There was no apparent reaction.

Stephanie finally looked in the rearview mirror. Was that Freddie following her? The nervy little bitch was coming to rub it in? Nah. Stephanie gunned the Honda anyway. Time to get out of the jerk's way.

"What's she doing?"

"Hell if I know." Freddie kept following her, several lengths behind. "What should I do?"

"Are you sure she saw you?"

"Fairly sure."

"Could something be bothering her?"

"Don't ask me questions like that. You remember the story. I'm the shameless hussy who could tell you more about the moles on her back than her moods."

"Are we getting closer? I think she turned off."

"Yeah. That's her place, all right."

"Okay. Pull over for a second, Freddie." Freddie did as she was told. "Let's just sit here for a few minutes and give her time to get into her place and settle down. I'm going to assume that she thought you were some pushy driver who was on her case for not going fast enough."

"You think so?"

"Either that, or she thinks you're my lover!" Sue laughed.

"Yeah, right." Freddie joined her laughing at the joke. Now that was truly ridiculous.

"We'll go knock on the door and straighten this out. I need to make myself a bit more presentable." Sue opened the door and crawled into the back seat to get into her carry-on case. She extracted a travel pack of wet towels and gave herself a quick sponge bath. "Okay, let's do this!"

"I could just as easily turn around, you know," Freddie offered.

"No, you couldn't. I'm here to protect you from yourself. If you didn't have two dozen afterthoughts for every thought, you'd probably know what she was thinking as well as where her moles were."

"Ouch."

"Time to tell it like it is, Freddie. You may think I was into proselytizing, but I was quite content to be the token lesbian in the family. I thought you were playing around or going through a phase. That was until I saw the look on your face at the thought of that woman in there in a pair of shorts. Now let's go in and knock on the door before you've changed your mind and she's changed her clothes." Sue had barely finished her last sentence before Freddie had the car in gear and was chugging up the last 300 feet to Stephanie's place.

ᴧᴥ   ᴧᴥ   ᴧᴥ

Stephanie threw her clothes in the laundry basket and grabbed a red T-shirt and a pair of sweat pants. The airport show had been too much for her. She had nearly killed herself getting home and then there was that stupid white car following her. Surely it wasn't the same idiot who was pressing her to pay already at the parking lot? It was definitely a touristmobile—white Chevy or Oldsmobile, something made in the USA.

Were all the stories she had told about the good-for-nothing husband a lie? Was Steve really a woman? Steve? Was that a butch nickname for Stephanie? *Christ, does she have one of us in each port? And that one was stepping out on her, so she decided to play dyke-virgin with me?*

She let the dog out. Pepper had barely finished relieving herself when she tore back in barking hysterically. Someone was knocking at the door. She stared through the peephole. *Oh, god.*

She opened the door in a stealth movement and looked at Freddie. Before the other woman could speak, Stephanie said, through gritted teeth, "I don't know what kind of game you're playing, but count me out. I quit." Stephanie glared for good measure.

Ooh, tough, thought Sue. *She's got it bad for Freddie.* Freddie seemed scared shitless of her, backing away in horror. Sue moved forward. "Susan Edelstein," she handed her a card, "Attorney-at-law." That ought to disarm her. Putting her title out there was her way of countering the flashy display of attitude and letting this one know that Freddie had backup. Why was she giving Freddie such a hard time? Sue could tell in five seconds that this moony stuff was mutual. What gave? Weird defense for all the sexual tension?

Stephanie turned sheet white. *She's got a lawyer. What is this, some sort of sexual misconduct suit? I didn't do anything wrong. She wanted to do it too.* Several different paranoid scenarios flashed across her mind simultaneously. This lawyer had such a strong New York accent. Was this whole thing orchestrated by Jill?

Sue decided to try a sweeter tactic. "I'm Freddie's cousin."

"Cousin? You're Freddie's cousin?"

Sue slapped her own forearm. "Could we take this little battle inside? Something's chewing on me out here."

"Come on in." Stephanie stepped aside. She motioned them in. They stood quite a bit apart, not as cozy as they'd been at the airport. Pepper, the little turncoat, treated the lawyer-cousin like a long lost best friend. "Pepper, this is Susan Edelstein, attorney-at-law," she said, introducing the dog in as sarcastic a hoity-toity voice as she could muster.

Stephanie turned to Freddie. "Why are you doing this to me, Freddie? First, you need time to think. We decide that you aren't going to talk to me. I try to break the ice again and you leave me a message saying that you want to keep the..." She hesitated. "...Cease-fire, shall we say, in place. Then you bring your cousin up here to meet me without giving me any warning? I look like shit and..."

"You could never look like shit. Did you, by any chance, listen to my other messages on your answering machine?"

"No."

You didn't listen to your answering machine, but you had time to change out of your shorts. Freddie looked deep into Stephanie's gold-flecked eyes, searching for something.

Stephanie wanted to back down, but she was so confused. She hated being this out of control. What about the mouth-to-mouth resuscitation number at the airport? She probably would have waved at or hugged a cousin. She couldn't even think of a cousin she'd feel compelled to kiss on the cheek. Logic be damned. Freddie had to be playing with her somehow. She hadn't exactly figured out what it was, but she was sure she was being toyed with.

"I know you're messing with my head. I just know it. How am I supposed to keep up with your mood swings?" Her voice was louder and angrier than she meant it to be.

"Freddie seems to be afraid of you, but I'm not. How about chilling out a little?"

"Great. Two against one," Stephanie snorted.

"I'm not against you. Yet."

Nobody was sitting. She hadn't really invited them to. Stephanie was still too uncomfortable to play the happy hostess.

She walked to the desk and rewound the answering machine. Freddie's recorded voice filled the room. Stephanie shivered. If she really screwed everything up, and she had a good start in that direction, she would at least have this tape to keep her warm at night. What a voice.

Freddie and Stephanie looked at each other for a long time. Sue finally broke the silence. "Look, I have to be in court a week from Thursday. Would one of you say something, for chrissake?" She turned to Stephanie and added, "Mind if I sit down. Didn't think so, thanks. By the way, nice T-shirt." Sue winked at Stephanie.

Freddie looked at the T-shirt. It was the "muff diving" shirt. The food stain was still there, bigger than life. She hadn't washed it since Freddie had worn it. Somehow, this small, slovenly gesture warmed her from head to toe. She moved toward Stephanie and took her hand. They stared at each other without speaking.

Sue finally let out an exasperated sigh and said, "She's crazy about you, you know. If she isn't going to say it, I will. I described you at the airport in your aloha shirt and shorts and she almost ran us off the road."

"You were checking me out. I knew it!" Stephanie's eyes widened as she flashed a knowing look at Sue.

"No, you were checking me out. I just thought you were giving out those...dyke vibes. I'm spoken for, anyway."

"Does your lover know that you suck face with your, quote, cousin, unquote, at airports?"

"What?" Freddie and Sue screeched simultaneously.

"What in the world are you talking about?" Freddie had let go of her hand and now had it on her own hip in an angry posture.

"You were all over each other at the airport, kissing each other on the mouth, your faces buried into one another."

"Were we at the same airport?" asked Sue. "Did we kiss on the mouth? You must be some lame kisser. Surely I would have remembered something like that," Sue teased.

"I wouldn't kiss you like that. Not intentionally. Maybe our lips brushed when I put the lei on you." Freddie's anger was quickly metamorphosing into amusement.

"Well, and that was a requirement." She tried desperately to cover the New Yorkese with a put-on hick accent. "Cuz, I'm gonna git me one of them 'I got leied in Hawaii' T-shirts at the Honolulu airport on my way home."

Stephanie laughed in spite of herself.

"You really thought we were lovers?" Freddie asked.

"Well, I said on the way over here that maybe she thought we were."

"Yeah, but you were kidding. She really thought that. I guess I did hug you for a while. I was crying and thanking you for coming here and stuff."

"And then there was the conversation in the bathroom," Stephanie reminded her.

"You were in the bathroom?"

"Yeah." She looked at Sue. "You said, 'so, why don't you just tell her?' And then Freddie said, 'I wasn't going to leave it on her answering machine. I'm just so relieved you came. I was going nuts.' I just assumed that I was some little diversion that helped heal whatever had gone wrong between you two and you were going to call me to say, 'It's been fun.'"

"It never occurred to you that those words could have a totally different meaning?" Sue asked.

"I'm sorry."

"Okay, Freddie, make nice and maybe she'll offer us something to drink."

"Yeah, Freddie. Make nice," Stephanie repeated. She ran her tongue over her teeth. Sue laughed.

Freddie stood still, suddenly feeling very shy. The four eyes cast on her felt like the spotlights of a huge stage. "Oh, Kole, I wanted to tell you that we needed to slow down, get to know each other better. I don't feel as confused as I did the other day. Sue here seems to get through life as a lesbian and she isn't nearly as mentally stable as I am..."

"This is the thanks I get for coming 5000 miles to do a good deed."

Stephanie walked into the kitchen. Freddie followed her. "Do you want something hard or soft?" she asked peering into the refrigerator. She looked back over and Freddie was laughing again. "I was talking about the drinks," she said. The words were barely out and they had their arms clasped around each other's waists in a warm embrace. They kissed tenderly and then again more passionately.

Freddie pulled back first. "Do you have any beer for Attila the Hun?"

"Yeah. What do you want...besides me?"

"Something soft."

Stephanie brought out the drinks and some Japanese sesame crackers and macnut cookies. Freddie settled back at her end of the couch. Rather than sit in a chair opposite them or sandwich herself between them, Stephanie sat on the floor in front of her, resting her head against Freddie's knees.

In the short time they had been gone, Sue had retrieved her notebook computer from the car and was typing madly. The sun was going down and the room was growing darker. Stephanie knew that she should probably stand up and turn on a lamp for Sue, but she didn't want to leave Freddie's lap.

Sue looked up at them. "This bizarre thing with the two of you has given me a great idea for a piece for the Lambda Legal Forum on the Internet. What do you think they'll do if they legalize same-sex marriage in several states? Will it still be illegal to marry your cousin? I mean, if you weren't a breeder, what would the problem be? Maybe we'll do one of those web page soap opera things." She began singing off-key, "They're cousins, identical cousins, and you'll find, they kiss alike, they hug alike..." She stopped singing. "I'll think of some more words and get back to you."

"Why don't you save it for one of your lesbian lawyer conferences?" Freddie offered.

"Yeah, and wait until everyone's had too much to drink," Stephanie muttered under her breath.

Freddie snickered and displayed a thumbs-up sign in front of Stephanie.

"Hey. This two against one stuff only works when I'm on the bigger team!" Sue said.

"She's always been a bully. When we were little she was always pulling my hair."

"You're still little!"

"Hmpf."

The click of Sue's computer keys was the only sound for several minutes. Freddie was kneading Stephanie's shoulders and Stephanie was wishing she could twitch her nose and make Sue disappear.

"You can cut the tension with a knife. Why don't you two go 'talk it out' in the other room," Sue suggested.

"I have to apologize for my cousin's manners, Steph. You know what they say: you can take the girl out of New York, but…"

"Woman," Sue corrected. "You can spew aphorisms and still be P.C."

"What I was trying to say is that she thinks this is her house and she can order us around."

Sue, barely looking up from the computer, pointed to the bedroom.

"I'd love to…talk," Stephanie murmured huskily. She stood up, put a Joan Armatrading CD on the player, and motioned Freddie into the bedroom.

Stephanie closed the door behind her and they melted into one another. They fell onto the bed and it made a sloshing sound as a small wave rippled through. They were laughing and groping, trying not to make much noise.

"I can't believe you haven't washed this shirt," Freddie said, tracing the food spot she had gotten on it the other day. Although the spot was low, it made Stephanie's nipples come to attention and become visible through the shirt. "You need a laundress. I may be available. I wash a mean load of clothes."

"I was planning to never wash this again. It smelled sweet…like you," she whispered back.

"Oh, Kole. Why are we so hard on each other?" her voice cracked from the semi-whisper.

"This is ridiculous. I feel like a teenager in the basement," Stephanie said.

"The basement felt further away than this does."

Stephanie pulled Freddie up off the bed and led her into the master bathroom. She kicked the door closed behind her. She put the lid down on top of the toilet and sat down. She sat Freddie on her lap, Freddie's back flush against her chest. Stephanie kissed her neck and ears leisurely and fondled her breasts.

Freddie shivered at the sensations. She shifted to sitting on one of Stephanie's knees, reached behind and wedged her hands into the waist-band of the baggy sweat pants. Stephanie gasped. Freddie worked her hands down between Stephanie's legs. Discovering a flood of sexual juices, she said, "I guess you were happy to see me."

"Uhmm hmm," Stephanie murmured.

They looked like a comedy team that used one person's face and the other's arms and legs, but there was nothing funny or awkward about the events that transpired. They were instantly in synch. Stephanie was rocking and gasping. She took one hand from Freddie's breast and turned the sink water on full blast.

"What are you doing?"

"I'm about to explode and I really don't want to share this with anyone else." Freddie quickened her finger dance and Stephanie soon bellowed and bucked in orgasm. The wail behind her was so loud that it actually depressed Freddie's left eardrum momentarily, like hitting a high floor on an elevator. Freddie climbed down from Stephanie's lap and rinsed her fingers in the running water before turning off the faucet.

Stephanie attempted to stand, but started to stagger. "She may suspect something if I can no longer walk."

"She has a real dirty mind, so she'll suspect something anyway."

Stephanie lifted the toilet seat and lowered her pants and her butt. She felt a bit shy using the john in front of Freddie. Wanting to tinkle in private was a silly last toehold before giving in to total intimacy. Between the excitement and the audience, Stephanie had forgotten how to pee.

Freddie walked back and kissed her. "I have the urge to kiss a woman who's about to pee."

I guess I needed a cheering squad! The kiss seemed to do the trick and she was able to relieve herself.

Freddie went back in the bedroom and plopped down on the bed. Stephanie came out of the bathroom and headed for Freddie.

She reached for Freddie's shorts. Freddie grabbed her hand. "We've been...uh...talking for a long time. I feel bad. She came a long way and she must be jet-lagged."

"Okay." Stephanie stood up and began to change out of her shirt and sweat pants.

"What are you doing?"

"What?"

"Don't change clothes. That would be really obvious..."

She assumed Sue knew what they were capable of left alone, but she didn't want to argue with Freddie anymore, not even about something small. They brushed their hair and helped smooth each other out, ready to present themselves once again in the living area.

As they came back in, Sue looked up from the computer and down again. "Anyone for a Lucky Strike?" she asked absently.

Freddie flushed. She was sure they couldn't be heard through two doors and the running water with the music playing.

Sue glanced back up and marveled at the color in her cousin's cheeks. "Come on Freddie, don't have a stroke. I'm a lawyer and a lesbian. I know what you honeymoon types do behind closed doors. I'm not reacting to anything specific, except that you both seem much calmer than you did before. I don't belong here. Do you have the hotel key on you? You could give me the car and some simple directions and I could get out of your hair. I have a pretty good sense of direction."

Freddie guffawed. "We'd have to put an APB out for her in Hilo if I let her out there by herself." Hilo was almost 100 miles away.

"There's a spare room," Stephanie offered.

"Naw. It looks like everything is pretty close together in here."

"Could Sue stay here and we go back to the hotel?"

"Well, sure. If she wants to. How does that sound? You'd have to let the dog out, though."

"No problem. We get along great, don't we, Peeper?"

"It's Pepper," Stephanie corrected.

"She knows. She's just trying to get your goat. She has an incredible memory, photographic. That's how she partied night and day and still graduated from law school."

"So, where does little Pooper sleep, anyway?"

"Endora? I was just having a little *Bewitched* fantasy myself. I was wishing I could twitch my nose and Freddie and I would be alone."

"Didn't you just love that character, though? Now Agnes Moorehead, she was a cool dyke."

"Agnes Moorehead was a lesbian?" Freddie questioned, innocently. They both looked at her incredulously.

"Come on, that was one of those shows where you needed to count the straight people first because that was the shorter list!" Stephanie volunteered.

The final configuration for two against one. The two lesbo pros against the newly initiated. "I guess I'm not up on that sort of trivia," Freddie pouted.

"You may need 'that kind of information' the way you're heading, Freddie! I can't believe I'm giving up a night in a hotel on my first vacation in two years in support of your new-found proclivities..."

"She has a waterbed."

"Whoa doggies! Did I give the impression I was complaining? Sorry. I'll have to call Nick and we can have phone sex. I love waterbeds."

Ordinarily, Freddie would have deemed that way too much information, but, at this point, who was she to criticize? Freddie gave her the keys to the rental car and told her not to drive anywhere unless there was a dire emergency. Stephanie gave her a house key, wrote down phone numbers and showed Sue how to work the TV and VCR. She explained where the cold cuts and bread were and they were finally on their way.

They were part way down the hill when Freddie spoke. "A lot of people find Sue a bit hard to swallow. She's a real friend, though. They say she's a damn good lawyer."

"She's fine. I wish I could have met her under calmer circumstances, though. You and I seem to bring out all the passionate neuroses in one another."

"Yeah. I know what you mean," Freddie agreed.

Stephanie swallowed hard before she asked the next question. "I really don't want to rock the boat, but how are you doing in the self-doubt department?"

"I had a lot of time to think today."

"And?"

"And that's why I called you back. I'm an analyzer. If I sit holed up somewhere thinking about whether or not I should be doing this, I'll 'what if' myself to death. I came up with the idea that it would help for us to slow down and then I saw you again and lost all of my reasoning powers. Whatever is going on between us has a mind of its own. There's some kind of magnetic pull. I can't fight it…I don't want to fight it."

"Neither do I."

"I want to be with you now. It feels right. I'm not sure what kind of guarantee I can make. I'd be lying if I didn't admit there's some flip-flopping going on in my head. I've always been kind of wishy-washy."

"You? I wouldn't have thought so."

"I may be more decisive about some things," she laughed. "Of course, I must be leaning in the obvious direction, or I wouldn't have let my big-mouthed cousin come to town. Given the chance, she'd be right there to convince me that if I were to return to, shall we say, business as usual, that I'd be the biggest fool on the planet." Freddie's voice was slightly shaky as she completed her thoughts.

"I went through a lot when I came out," Stephanie told her. "It really isn't that strange. I've met some women who told me they knew all their lives, but I don't think it's that unusual to be confused. After my first time with a woman, I had a mélange of garbage to work out in my mind."

"About what?" Freddie asked.

"About who I was. I thought I might be bisexual. I tried to convince myself that there had to be some man who could excite me like that. It took a while, but I learned to accept myself in stages. I think the key is maintaining balance. Think things through, try not to over-analyze it to the point that you're left with nothing." *Did that sound threatening?*

The words made sense to Freddie. "You're really something, Stephanie. You're wise, you're beautiful, and you're kind."

"You're just saying that to get on my good side," Stephanie laughed. She put her arm across Freddie's lap. "I was worried about you getting blue ovaries. I wasn't finished with you back there."

"I'll let you pick up where you left off when we get back to the hotel."

They were still up above town. Stephanie made a sudden turn on a dirt road and drove to a deserted area. She parked and leaned over to nuzzle Freddie's neck. Freddie kissed her cheek. "Come on. Let's go look at the stars."

As Freddie got out, she heard the trunk pop. Stephanie pulled a blanket out of the trunk, closed the trunk and spread the blanket over the back of the car. She lifted Freddie up and then herself. They leaned back and gazed at the stars. "This is beautiful," Freddie whispered.

"You're beautiful," Stephanie corrected.

They kissed briefly. "Do you always travel with a blanket in the trunk?"

"Yeah. I was a Girl Scout. I'm always prepared."

Stephanie lowered herself off the trunk and pushed Freddie's legs apart. "This is where I left off," she said, sliding Freddie's shorts and sticky underwear off and nuzzling her head between her thighs.

Freddie tried to keep her eyes open and watch the stars, but her vision became blurry as she felt any semblance of control slip away. The climax came in huge waves. She cried out, "Oh, Kole... Oh, Kole."

When Stephanie was once again lying at her side on the blanket, she kissed her, giving Freddie a full taste of herself. Stephanie lifted her head up and said in a sly voice, "You really have to stop calling me an asshole in public."

Neither of them moved for several minutes. "How are you doing?" Stephanie whispered.

"I'm...fine," said Freddie, her voice quavering.

Damn. Stephanie swallowed. "I have this sneaking suspicion that you're not just trembling from the throes of passion. Can we look for some sort of master switch to throw so you can stop revisiting all those doubts in your mind?"

"I'm not sure that is scientifically possible, but if it were and you knew how, we could surely market it and make a fortune," Freddie answered, her voice growing stronger.

"In fact, it comes in bottles and I could use one right about now."

"I'm sorry I'm so transparent. Sue tells me she can actually hear the wheels turning when I get pensive."

"I have a feeling that I will live to regret this, but what are you thinking about?"

"Last night, I got online and read the current research on the 'gay gene' and latent homosexuality."

A derisive snort slipped out before Stephanie could control herself. "Come to any conclusions?"

"Not exactly."

"I know that you like to dissect everything, but can't you just be in the moment with me, here, Freddie?" Stephanie pushed to curb the edginess to her voice to no avail. She took a deep breath. "Close your eyes and let's try a little experiment."

Freddie obliged. It was a conundrum. She felt a pressing need to share her thoughts with Stephanie, but she knew some of the mental table tennis would not meet with Stephanie's approval.

"I want you to imagine that money, time, or the entire time-space continuum, for that matter, are no object. You can be anywhere, with anyone, at this moment." Stephanie paused for effect. "Where do you want to be?"

"Here." Freddie had amazed herself—there had been no mental debate, no hesitation and no forlornness in her response. Surely this woman was a sorceress. "You've cast some sort of spell over me."

"I wish that were true. Since I'm on some sort of roll here, let me ask you something else." Stephanie pushed on, "If you had winked at some guy that night in the bar and you were telling your cousin the same story with lots of he's instead of she's, what would have been different?"

"I can't imagine…"

"What?"

"I just can't even imagine it."

"Me, either, Freddie. Doesn't that tell you something? The question isn't just how you could have had the propensity to become a damn fine lesbian all these years and not known about it. It's more than that. You are questioning the universe. What attracts anyone to anyone? Why do I feel that I have known you for decades, when we can't even count it in weeks? Why does the air crackle every time I get within two feet of you? And, yes, again, if you have the answers to any of these questions, we could go on the lecture circuit and become rich and famous. I know society has you in a tizzy about our being the same sex, but, really, Freddie, why does anyone desire anyone? Why do I want you in a way I have never wanted another person before?"

Why, indeed? Maybe Stephanie had been wasting her time as a photographer. She was an impressive lecturer. Although they were silent in the car, Stephanie's words replayed in Freddie's ears all the way back to the hotel.

They prepared for bed in a light, pleasant manner, as if they had been doing it their entire lives. Neither of them wore nightclothes.

They met in the center of the king-size bed and snuggled into one another, falling asleep cuddled together.

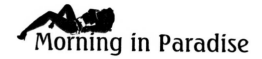

Morning in Paradise

MOST OF STEPHANIE AWOKE BEFORE her right arm. Freddie's head was pinning it to the bed. Awake she looked like a kewpie doll, but asleep she looked like a cherub. The lines of her face were relaxed, giving her a youthful and peaceful appearance. The numbness was moving from her arm to her shoulder. *I know I said I'd give my right arm for a relationship like this, but wasn't that just a figure of speech?* When she'd finally decided she couldn't stand it and would have to move, Freddie's eyes fluttered open, as if on cue.

"Good morning," Freddie yawned, rolling off Stephanie's arm.

"Good morning, baby," Stephanie cooed, massaging her own shoulder.

"Something wrong with your shoulder? Want me to rub it?" Stephanie didn't have to be asked twice. She was instantly prone and enjoying the warmth and precision of Freddie's nimble little fingers. Stephanie moaned with pleasure.

"Is there anything I can do that doesn't garner this reaction?"

"Probably not. Did I tell you that when I first heard your voice on the phone it made me wet?"

"No," Freddie said her throat catching slightly. Stephanie rolled over and pinned her down, kissing her face and neck. "You know, this is the first time I ever slept naked all night," Freddie confessed.

"What?" Stephanie laughed. "You mean to tell me that in all your... How old are you exactly?"

"Forty."

"In all your forty years, you never slept naked all night?"

"No. I'd always get dressed again before going to sleep."

"I'm flattered to be your first all night nude encounter. And I'm glad you're forty. It's perfect. We're both in the prime of our sexual peaks! And since you're the one with the fancy degree, I wanted to be the older one."

"So, how old are you?"

"Forty-one in August."

"Then you're still forty."

"Yeah, but I already think of myself as forty-one."

"I'll be forty-one in December. Congratulations, you're four months older. Do you really have a thing about my degree?"

"No, I don't have a 'thing' about your degree. I do have a thing about you, though. I just am amused that you, and your cousin, for that matter, start every new acquaintance with 'Here's my business card—see, I went to school forever.'"

"You're exaggerating!"

"Not by much."

Freddie thought about it for a minute. She wondered about Stephanie's background. How would she phrase the question? Wasn't there quite a range of possible educational backgrounds for a professional photographer—from the "school of hard knocks" all the way to advanced degrees? The phone jangled before she could think of a clever way to shift the conversation to Stephanie's background.

Stephanie pulled herself up and let Freddie get the phone.

"Hello. ...Yeah. It's 11:00? Sorry... Just a second." She pushed the mouthpiece of the receiver to her chest to muffle it. "Sue's ranting and raving. She's been up since 4:30 because of the jet lag, and she's wondering when we'll have our okoles in gear."

"Why doesn't she come here and have brunch with us? Wouldn't you trust her to drive in now that she's better rested? It's pretty much just straight down the hill. I give great directions." Freddie handed her the phone.

While Stephanie explained the way to the hotel to Sue, Freddie brushed her teeth and washed her face. Just as she was patting her face dry, Stephanie came into the bathroom. She started to brush her teeth with toothpaste on her finger. Freddie left her and rummaged through her suitcase. She came back to the bathroom brandishing an unopened toothbrush. "You aren't the only Girl Scout!"

"Thanks."

"I thought you bohemian types always shared toothbrushes, anyway."

"Some people find that kind of gross. I didn't want to overstep the boundaries."

"Uh-huh. I see. Have I ever refused you anything?" Freddie asked dramatically.

"Faye Dunaway. *Three Days of the Condor*. I love Faye Dunaway in that film."

"Until a few days ago, I would have sworn that I'd been watching for Robert Redford. Do you want the shower first?"

Stephanie didn't respond. She just started the water and helped Freddie into the tub. She stood with one leg propped up on the bathtub ledge and washed Freddie's back. Without the security of the stall at home, Stephanie was very careful that neither of them slipped. They took turns under the shower soaping and scrubbing one another from the side of the tub. The hotel towels, however, were not big enough for the Turkish bath human rubdown that they'd enjoyed at Stephanie's. Stephanie grabbed a towel and let herself out of the bathroom to enjoy some cooler air. Freddie lingered for several minutes over lotions and other rituals of ablution and perfuming. When Freddie emerged, Stephanie was sitting on the edge of the bed brushing her wet hair.

Freddie sat down beside her and massaged her damp neck. "How's your shoulder?"

"It's better. I'm a little stiff. It happens. I call it 'waterbed withdrawal.'"

"Has anyone ever told you how witty and articulate you are?"

"You mean for someone without a 'fudd' at the end of her name?"

There it was again. Freddie's first instinct was to prod her into explaining what her issues really were about Freddie having advanced degrees. The playful glint in those big eyes, however, made her act like a moth committing suicide by flying into a streetlight. Freddie bent her face towards her and kissed her softly on the lips. She pushed herself on top of Stephanie and began a full force assault, attempting a tonsillectomy with her tongue. Stephanie was panting when Freddie finally released her. Freddie catapulted herself off Stephanie and calmly asked, "So, what time did you tell Sue?"

"Oh, no you don't," Stephanie said pulling her back on top of her. "I told her 12:30, which gives me a full forty-five minutes to have my way with you." Incapable of resistance, Freddie's willing body became limp and pliable. "Do you realize that if you count the number of times we've made love," Stephanie continued, "our percentage of time spent on an actual bed is quite low? I was fixing to even up those figures."

"You have a one track mind."

"Oh? And what were you thinking about?" Stephanie asked. She flipped Freddie over onto her back and was on her knees over her, kissing her face. She untwisted Freddie's towel and opened it up to feast on her nipples. Her own towel had fallen off and was missing in action.

With Stephanie's breasts undulating in front of her, Freddie alternately tweaked each nipple. She reached her left hand towards Stephanie's right buttock, but couldn't quite get her fingers around her hip and beyond. Freddie noticed the hairbrush on the nightstand and picked it up. It gave her the extra five inches she wanted. She tapped Stephanie on the butt with the plastic bristles of the brush.

"Ooh, are we playing that game again? Spank me, Teach, I've been very bad," Stephanie responded appropriately. For someone who had never role-played in bed and had rarely strayed from the missionary position, Freddie learned fast. The brush became a massage tool and a dildo. When Stephanie snatched it and used it to brush her pubic hair, the ticklish sensation sent Freddie into spasms of pleasure.

By 12:27 they were hosing themselves down in the bathroom once again and giggling like two schoolgirls. The initiation ceremony to their private club involved trading toothbrushes for one last polish before they had to incorporate the rest of the world into their day.

And the Beat Goes On

THEY DECIDED ON SUSHI FOR lunch. The restaurant was practically empty. The owner nodded to Stephanie, a semi-regular. She offered them water and said that the California Rolls were specially priced that week.

"*Genchi no mono nara nani ga oishiideshooka?*"

"*Nihongo umai nee... opakapaka toiu shiromi ga saikoo oishiidesuyoo.*"

"She's just showing off. Did she tell you she lived in Japan?" Sue asked.

"Just in passing."

"She said the *opakapaka* was really good," Freddie reported.

"I could've told you that. It's a local pink snapper. You never told me what you were doing in Japan."

"Oh. I taught science at the American School in Japan for a few years. Good job. I liked it a lot. They hired both of us, actually. Steve's a history teacher. We freelanced there, too. I taught English a few hours a week at a local university and he taught some company executives. We used the money we saved to buy the house in L.A."

The mention of L.A. made Stephanie feel sick. Not only had they exchanged very little personal information, but also nobody had broached the subject of how long Freddie planned to stay in Hawaii.

"How'd you end up here in Kona?" Sue asked Stephanie.

"Some friends from New York settled in Hilo and I got a few leads on jobs here. A couple of summers before, we'd been here on vacation and we went diving and snorkeling quite a bit. I had really good luck selling my underwater photographs, so I wanted to try living here. My lover, uh, my ex-lover is a jewelry designer, so we didn't have a lot of business ties to New York. It seemed like a good move. It's peaceful and beautiful here. Real estate is much more reasonable than on Oahu. We would have joined our friends in Hilo, which is even cheaper, but I couldn't see having to drive for a couple of hours every time I needed to take some good underwater shots or visit the galleries."

"Maybe we have friends in common. You don't sound like a New Yorker, though."

"No. I'm originally from the Midwest. I've lived in Illinois, Ohio, and Indiana, so my accent is as flat as the landscape there."

Freddie listened intently. Sue was a good buffer. It seemed as if Freddie and Stephanie couldn't talk much without the conversation being charged with questions of intent or interfering hormones.

Sue turned to Freddie and brushed her cheek with one finger. "I guess it's true what they say about constant sex being good for your complexion. That acne has really cleared up." Freddie turned red and made fists with both hands. "Don't you just love how easy it is to tease her?"

If only you knew, thought Stephanie, *if only you knew*. Stephanie put her hands over Freddie's and smoothed out the fists. They exchanged a warm glance.

"At least I won't have to be a third wheel for much longer. Nick is on the 4:21 flight."

"Huh? Nicki's coming here? I thought she was working on some huge project."

"She is, but their grant money finally came through, so she can work on her research online and send in updates by e-mail. I told her to book the one that gets here at 4:21 from Honolulu. I had a really long layover in Honolulu."

"Nicki, her...friend," Freddie began, consciously avoiding the term *lover*, "does psychological research." Stephanie was watching her closely and it made Freddie squirm. The thought of invading Stephanie's world with yet another person, especially another person with a lah dee dah education, was troubling.

"Sounds like it's going to be a party," Stephanie said cheerfully. "Why don't you and Sue do something fun this afternoon and give me a chance to get the house straightened up and my appointment book up to date? We can have pupus on the lanai and then all go out to dinner." She turned to Sue. "Where are you staying?"

"I don't know. Since it's not high season, I figured something would be available. You think your hotel has vacancies, Freddie?"

Stephanie turned to Freddie. "Aren't you on some kind of package? Why don't you give them your room and stay at the house with me?"

Freddie shuddered.

Was it excitement or fear? Stephanie held her breath. Everything had been going so well today. Why did she always have to push?

"Are we having our second date?" Freddie asked in a meek voice.

Stephanie grinned. *Thank you, God.* "Looks that way. Remind me to tell you something later."

Regrouping: Freddie and Sue

THEY HAD COME TO THE restaurant in Stephanie's Honda, but since the hotel was only three blocks away, Sue and Freddie opted to walk back and check out the shops along the way.

"How are you doing?"

"Okay. We talked a little last night." They walked into a shop and looked at T-shirts. Sue held one or two up to her chest and put them down again.

"Good." There was a pregnant pause that caused Sue to snort.

"What?" They walked back out on the street.

"I'm supposed to be supportive and you and I are family, so I don't feel like I should be pushing you."

Yes, you've been exercising so much self-control. "But you'd love details."

"More information would be nice, yes."

They stopped in another shop and Sue spun the postcard rack. She looked over a few with topless women and another featuring three women in string bikinis, hip to hip, sand clinging to pale cheeks contrasting with tanned thighs. Freddie looked at the card over Sue's shoulder. "Nah," Sue decided and put the cards back on the rack.

"Why do you think I'd be willing to share details? Do I ask what you and Nicki do behind closed doors?" They were back on the street.

"I wasn't asking whose hand went where or anything like that. I want to know what you're feeling. I've hardly had any time to talk to you. We spent all that time tailing her and then you had your little make-up, or was it make-out, session, and you were off."

"I thought one of the ground rules was that you weren't going to make me feel cheap."

"Ah-ha. You have more reasons to feel cheap."

"No shit, Sherlock."

"She's ba-ack!"

"Huh?"

"You're very demure around Stephanie. Your voice is always quiet and you don't swear."

"Get out!"

"I think it's kind of cute." They walked into the ice cream shop. The boy who had been told to "get off his okole and get back to work" smiled at her in recognition.

They each had a scoop of macnut chocolate ripple ice cream in a cup. They sat at a table in the corner. "You look good together. Kind of got that Mutt and Jeff thing going."

"Mutt and Jeff, ha! Now there's a reference that dates you. You think she's too tall for me?"

"Nah. Maybe you're too short for her, though. She's a knockout. Like something that stepped out of one of those Amazon sexpot comic books."

Freddie played with the image for a moment. She imagined Stephanie running down the street in a satin crime-fighting outfit making the world safe for democracy. The image both amused and titillated her.

"You know, Freddie, I knew both of the schmucks you were married to. I was at both weddings and in both houses. I saw you do the good little housewife number on countless occasions. I even remember your boyfriend from high school. I've been around for most of the big relationships in your life. And I never, ever, saw you look at anyone the way you've been looking at this woman."

There it was in a nutshell. "I know."

She paused. "You can do this, Freddie, if it's what you want."

"We need to get to know each other better. The physical attraction is so strong that…we don't talk much." *So much for keeping it all to myself.*

This revelation made Sue's eyes widen slightly. "Uh-huh."

"She's made a bunch of jokes about my degree. It's on my business card. Actually, she said it ran in the family. The way you gave her your title at the door."

"Hey, I was trying to protect you and distract her. She seemed kind of out of control. I could tell from her reaction that she thought you'd brought me over there to sue her for something."

"Really? I was so caught up in trying to figure out what made her so angry that I didn't even pick up on that. I've put her through even more crap than I realized. Poor baby."

"Have you used the 'L-word' yet?"

"You mean...l-l-lesbian?" Freddie stammered.

"No, Bozo. I was thinking of l-l-love."

"No." Not out loud, anyway.

"Has she asked how long you're in town for?"

"No. We've successfully avoided all of these verbal land mines. We just..."

"I know. You don't want to talk about it, but you've been too busy breaking some kind of land-speed record for multiple orgasms to have any of the expected conversations."

"I won't lie and deny having a lot of great sex, but I don't think we were too busy to talk about this stuff. I'd say we were too afraid."

Reunion

STEPHANIE SCRUBBED EVERYTHING DOWN INSIDE the house. She even ran the hose on the windows from the outside. She moved stacks of magazines and clothes to their more proper places.

Pepper chased the vacuum cleaner around as if it were a small animal. Since Jill left, Stephanie had not been particularly compulsive about housecleaning, which had given Pepper time to forget what the vacuum cleaner was for. Granted, she had been sweeping and dusting on a regular basis and Sue and Freddie had already experienced her tolerance for clutter, but she was officially "entertaining" this time and she wanted the place to look its best.

There were two calls on her answering machine. Both were offering work. She was more excited about being asked to take photos at the volcano than substituting for the videographer on the snorkel cruise, but she was happy to have a variety of work. She returned both calls.

In order to discourage mosquitoes from attending their cocktail party, she lit a Japanese mosquito coil ahead of time. She even made it out to the edge of the yard and dusted off and treated the spa. Once Jill had left town, she had stopped using the hot tub. After moving to Kona, the spa was the only place they had been civil to one another outside of an occasional tumble on the waterbed.

Jill. The relationship had been the opposite of what she was experiencing with Freddie. In the beginning, they were friends who talked and talked. A few months after they met, Jill had told her that she had mourned her deceased lover for a year and a half and finally, she was ready to date again. Two nights later, she and Stephanie had shared a bottle of wine and fallen into bed. Thus began her longest relationship to date. The sex was reasonable, although it had tapered off quite a bit in the last year they were together.

To her delight, getting the hot tub going again hadn't been as much of a hassle as she anticipated. She covered it and set the controls. She was hoping that she and Freddie would climb into the hot tub later, after dinner. Stephanie had made reservations at a nice quiet restaurant just steps from the ocean. If Sue's girlfriend ended up being too tired for someplace a little special, she had reasoned they could cancel and go to a pizza place.

She decided on vegetarian pupus. She hadn't asked about anybody's eating habits. She'd seen Freddie and Sue eat shrimp, but she wasn't sure if anybody ate beef or pork, so she decided against adding pepperoni slices to the cheese platter. She had bought some edible rice paper, Asian pickles, bean sprouts and mint at the supermarket with the plan to make vegetable roll-ups. All she needed to do was make sure the veggies were cut up and the sprouts washed ahead of time. Vegetable roll-ups were an interactive appetizer that everyone made for herself. Stephanie preferred to entertain where guests had lots of choices and participated in the process.

She had the ceiling fans on high blast, but it was more humid than usual; the trade winds must not have been up to par. She opened all of the screened windows and dusted and cleaned the windowsills. She also attacked some of the baseboards. The geckos helped by eating some of the insects, but they also tended to leave their droppings here and there.

The place was surely up to passing casual inspection. Besides, it was much too hot for anyone to be wearing white gloves. It was 4:50. She looked over her house one more time. There was a towel tied to the freezer door—her culinary string-around-the-finger trick. Shoot. She'd been quick chilling some wine and forgotten all about it. She extracted two bottles from the freezer and saw that they were just slightly crystallized. She transferred them to the bottom of the refrigerator.

She rummaged in a kitchen drawer looking for cheese knives. Before she came to them, she found a kitchen timer. "There you are," she said aloud, putting the timer on the kitchen counter. The location of this particular device had eluded her when she was chilling the wine. She unearthed two European cheese knives and washed them off to set out with the cheese platter. Now everything was clean, tidy, and ready—except for her.

After a quick shower, she dressed in a long, sleek, strapless Hawaiian dress. She stepped outside and plucked a small orchid, which she placed behind one ear.

Leilani showed up at 5:15 with three leis, presents for the guests. Stephanie paid her for today's goods as well as for the basket she had ordered for Freddie the other day.

"Sounds like you got plenty company lately!" she said in the local vernacular.

"Yeah, plenty." As far as Stephanie could ascertain, 'plenty' was the number after two in Hawaii. She thanked Leilani and walked her back to her car.

She'd just finished rearranging the pillows on the sofa when the white Ciera pulled up. Freddie had called to check in and they had decided that the best way to keep Nicki in the time zone was to keep her awake, so dinner at the nice place was a "go." Stephanie had mentioned that she tended to dress up a bit for this particular restaurant. Sue and Nicki were sitting in the back seat. Stephanie bit her lip in anger. They had only been apart for two days. It was totally rude to treat your cousin like the chauffeur just to be able to fondle your lover in the back seat.

Sue opened the front passenger seat and extracted a huge flower arrangement. "Hey there, Stephanie. This is for you." She handed her the flowers. Stephanie set them in the doorway.

"Thank you. They're magnificent." *Sorry I was so quick to judge you.*

"This is my Nicki," she said gesturing as Nicki scrambled around the car to greet her. Stephanie was barely looking at either of them as she watched Freddie emerge from behind the wheel. She had on a short dress with a low scoop neck and Empire waist. There was a lot of creamy shoulder showing, and Stephanie thought her knees might buckle if she took a step. Freddie caught sight of her with the flower behind her ear and winked at her. This time, there would be no passing it off as a nervous twitch.

"Oh, sorry," Stephanie said, turning back to Sue and her friend. She put the lei around Sue's neck and gave her a peck on the cheek.

She approached Nicki. "Nice to…" The other woman was staring at her with her mouth open. Freddie had caught up to them. "Colette?"

"Colette?" Sue and Freddie repeated in unison.

"Professor Amalfi?"

"Professor Amalfi??" It was the cousins again.

"*The* Professor Amalfi?" Sue asked Nicki. Nicki blushed and nodded.

Freddie could feel all the color rush to her face. *What's this "professor" stuff?* Stephanie is some famous professor that even Sue has heard of? She felt like slapping Nicki. She was staring at Stephanie. Was it awe or lust? And look at Stephanie; she was eating it up. *Chu, chu,* she would slap them both. *Colette?* Of course; Nicki's full name was Nicolette. Freddie had cleared up one mystery.

Without further explanation, Stephanie put the lei on Nicki and said, "Welcome to Hawaii, Colette."

"This is for you, baby," she breathed and put the lei on Freddie with a chaste kiss on each side of her face.

Afraid to kiss me in front of "Colette?" Sure, you've already welcomed me to Hawaii.

They were instructed to remove their shoes at the door and were ushered to the tiled lanai through the living area. The place sparkled. Either ServiceMaster had an emergency number or Stephanie had been very busy.

After the wine had been poured and they were sitting around the patio table, Sue leaned over and grinned at Stephanie. "Well, I guess I have you to thank for Nicki," Sue said conspiratorially. "She had the biggest crush on you. She always says that after your class, she knew she loved women."

What did you do? Diddle her in the darkroom? Freddie cycled through a series of catty thoughts and imagined realities. She took a gulp of the wine to anesthetize the pain in her gut. Why on earth was she so jealous that it hurt?

"She used to screw up her F-stops on purpose, just to get you to lean over and fix her camera for her." Freddie could see that Nicki looked just as uncomfortable as she felt.

"I thought the young women did that 'dizzy' routine to convince all the young men on campus that they were helpless femmes fatales. I'm flattered to think it was for my benefit. I barely knew I was a lesbian back then, though. When were you in my class, Colette?"

"It must have been 1978. I was a sophomore."

Perfect. Sounds like you were pretty sophomoric. Freddie attempted to lose the frown that had taken up residence on her face.

"And then you must have been in the 'Shooters Club.' Were you still there when we had the museum showing?"

"Yeah, I remember how excited you were."

Freddie was digging her nails into the lanai furniture. Her cheeks felt hot. Too much wine? Too much nostalgia about the horny coed with the camera? Stephanie was looking at her.

"You feeling okay, Freddie?"

Freddie? Was she too shy to call her kewpie doll or some other sweet name, as she had in front of Sue earlier? "Fine," she managed.

Until twenty minutes ago, she would have said she liked Nicki. Freddie wanted to be somewhere else. Nicki was fawning over Stephanie, who was enjoying the attention to no end. Sue had to be plotting ways to use the photography teacher and the naughty college student routine in bed that night. Or worse. Hadn't they once told her something about a threesome? Last year when she was visiting, they had stayed up very late and there was some covert reference to a woman named Fern and the three of them in a hot tub.

"When did you become 'Nicki'?" Stephanie asked.

"Right after I graduated. The first time I went to one of the bars, I told someone my name was Nicki. It seemed less pretentious than Colette and less of a mouthful than Nicolette."

"I told her she should use the whole thing as much as possible. Nicolette is such a pretty name," Sue said.

"I use it on all my research documents, of course."

"What kind of research do you do? I seem to remember you were majoring in journalism."

Stephanie crossed her long legs under the dress. Freddie wondered if it was a sexual signal to Nicki. *'I've been known to fuck people I met a few hours ago. You've wanted me all these years, let's lose the other two and head for my waterbed.'*

"I worked at a magazine for five years and then went back to school. I'm just finishing up graduate work in psychology. My research has to do with the effect of color on the human psyche."

Stephanie was nodding and beaming. *What, no Ph.D. jokes, Professor Amalfi? Or are those just reserved for me?*

"Interesting. You always had an eye for color composition," Stephanie remarked.

"She has a great memory, just like you, babe," Nicki said to Sue. Sue smiled and fondled Nicki's fingers.

After a beat, Sue changed the subject. "You know, I've been meaning to ask you. What's the community like here?"

"There are monthly brunches and social activities. I've got some friends from the Mainland who live near Hilo. There's quite a lesbian enclave where they are. There are some women's B&Bs on the Hilo side, too. I hear that the community organizes dances a couple times a year. And, I know a couple of women not far from here, in Captain Cook. I prefer living over here for the work, but I don't know many lesbians on this side. I don't usually make it to the brunches, so I really can't say much about what it's really like."

Sue and Nicki were nodding as if Stephanie were reading poetry rather than running down the lesbian scene on the Big Island. Freddie shifted uncomfortably in the patio chair.

"Maybe if someone planned some different activities here, more lesbians would surface on this side," Nicki offered. Sue and Stephanie nodded their heads in agreement.

Freddie attempted to join the conversation, but couldn't think of a thing to say, so instead she gritted her teeth. Stephanie glanced over at her and frowned at the pained look on her face. Freddie managed a weak smile.

Their discussion was a source of discomfort for her. It was all happening so fast the doubts were creeping back up over Freddie in droves. Was she in over her head? It wasn't just going to be about loving Stephanie. There was a new set of rules and values that came with this whole gay thing.

Everything was just starting to feel calmer between her and Stephanie. When rising to the challenge meant something more than lifting her behind off the bed, just what kind of lesbian was Freddie going to be? Was there a membership card? Could somebody throw you out for not toeing the party line? She'd met some of Sue's radical friends. They had barely tolerated her as a straight woman. They surely would have her for breakfast as someone who did the wild thing with women and couldn't list up the issues and spout the politics.

As Freddie drifted in and out she could hear them talking about gay congressional representatives and the status of same-sex marriages. Sue furnished the legal perspective. Nicki had migrated her puppy-dog gaze to Sue. She seemed to have a thing for professional women. An interesting turn-on...Freddie imagined Nicki watching documentaries and press conferences with professional females giving their opinion and becoming aroused—a heck of a lot cheaper than having to pay for the Playboy channel!

She was suddenly wracked with guilt. Was her discontent less about the lesbian lifestyle and the fact that Nicki and Stephanie knew each other and more about finding out that Stephanie was a professional woman? Did this make Stephanie less of a complete opposite of Steve? She'd done a complete mental comparison and they were opposites in every way she could think of. Steve was short and hirsute. Steve was also nerdy and academic. Had she been happier when she thought Stephanie might be some high school dropout with a good eye and an expensive camera?

Was this just "acting out?" *Steve nails his little chippy secretary, so I one-up him by bedding a female photographer that I barely know. One-upmanship? Hmm...more like one-hundred-upmanship. Surely carrying on a homosexual affair with a woman you just met would trump that cheating bastard's ace and then some.* There was definitely an overstock of mixed metaphors in her mind.

The mental ricochet of point-counterpoint was making her tired. Why was she thinking about Steve now? She'd barely given him a thought in the past two days. When she'd gone back to the hotel, they'd handed her the fifth message to call him with her key. She'd tossed it in the same trashcan in front of the elevator where she'd placed the first four.

Maybe it was the ultimate ego trip. *Hey, I can't schmooze about lesbian issues and I don't know any good bars, but I'm one hot shit—I have both men and women pining after me.* When she looked up, Nicki and Stephanie were once again engaged in animated conversation. *Did I say pining after me? I meant cheating after me. I'm the original bisexual doormat. Wipe your feet on old Freddie, regardless of your gender.*

"Freddie?" It was Sue speaking. No response. "Uh-oh," she said to Stephanie, "you have to be very careful when she goes into one of these trances. She'll have whole arguments with you in her head and blame you for something she imagined you saying."

Nicki and Stephanie laughed at this.

"Freddie?" Stephanie tried.

"Huh?" She was back.

"Could you give me a hand in the kitchen, Freddie, please?" Stephanie asked.

"Yeah." Freddie had worked her way up to slow boil. *I'll give you a hand, all right.*

They got into the kitchen. "What's the matter, honey?" Steph asked her. Now she was "honey." "Is it too much 'lifestyle' talk?"

Stephanie reached for Freddie's hand. It was freezing.

"I…" Freddie started to explain herself, but couldn't. The words were stopped just before her tongue. *I'm wildly jealous of anyone else even looking at you. I want to know why you made me feel embarrassed about my education. I want to hear about your life as a professor. I want you to help me clean out some of the rubbish in my head the way you cleaned this place up for this gathering. But first, I want to…*

Stephanie was warming Freddie's hand and moving closer. Stephanie bent her head towards her and Freddie could smell the wine on her breath. They kissed. Freddie sucked Stephanie's tongue and pushed her own into Stephanie's mouth with renewed passion. Stephanie's ragged breath encouraged Freddie to pursue her more aggressively. She dislodged the flower from behind Stephanie's ear as she ran her nails through her hair. Stephanie lowered her head and nibbled at the amply exposed neck and bare shoulders while Freddie trailed her fingers down Stephanie's back and caressed her hips. At this moment, Freddie hated the intruders from New York even more. She wanted to be alone with Stephanie. As she had promised, Stephanie was the antidote to the mental jumble. Freddie didn't have to think when she was with her; she just had to be.

Stephanie giggled and said, "This'll have to wait until later, kewpie doll." She retrieved the flower and repositioned it behind her ear. She looked at her reflection in the top oven door to smooth back her hair. She rinsed her hands off in the kitchen sink and then gathered up the ingredients for the vegetable roll-ups and put them on a tray that she handed Freddie. "I warmed up the hot tub for later," she whispered.

Freddie groaned inwardly. *Am I still not enough for her? Do I need to find out her views on orgies? Would Sue and Nicki ever leave if they found out that oh, great, beautiful, sexy, talented 'Professor' Amalfi has a waterbed **and** a hot tub?*

The vegetable roll-ups received "oohs" and "ahs."

"I brought you a present from New York," Nicki said to Freddie. She rummaged through her briefcase and dislodged a gift box, which she handed to Freddie.

"Maybe you should wait and open it later," Sue said forcefully. Freddie searched her eyes. "It's what we call the coming-out Pandora's-box-gift-set."

"Once you open it, poof, ye shall inherit the naughty lifestyle forever!" Nicki teased. The box slipped out of Freddie's shaky grip and hit the floor.

"This is a big adjustment for her," Stephanie said as she and Freddie nearly banged heads attempting to retrieve the box from the floor. "You shouldn't tease her like that, Colette."

Yeah, Colette, Freddie thought, suppressing the urge to stick out her tongue at her.

"Why don't you open it later? Actually, it's a little assortment for both of you," Sue told them.

﹏﹏ ﹏﹏ ﹏﹏

The restaurant was the most romantic place Freddie had ever seen. There were only about ten tables and the ocean was lapping at the rocks in front of them. The appetizers sounded wonderful, but the pupus at Stephanie's had already taken care of that. Everyone ordered local fish dishes and salads.

The salads were exotic combinations with garnishes of local Puna goat cheese and slices of Kula tomatoes. As they finalized their order, Sue expressed appreciation that arugula and balsamic vinegar were among the salad ingredients.

Stephanie confessed, "I could tell when I saw you at the airport that you were a Yuppie Dyke, so I thought that this restaurant would meet with your approval." Freddie tittered at the reference.

Sue sat facing her partner, putting Stephanie and Freddie out of touching range. They had the best table. It was close to the ocean and not very close to the other tables. It was covered in an elegant long tablecloth that practically touched the ground. The server seemed to know Stephanie and was friendly and efficient, yet didn't hover over them. After sharing some warm bread and olives, Sue and Nicki had gotten up and moved over to the edge of the terrace to look down at the ocean.

Being left alone in a darkness that was only slightly interrupted by candles illuminating the food compelled them to be daring. Stephanie moved her chair ever so slightly closer to the table and beckoned Freddie to do the same. There was a slight clacking noise under the table. Freddie's eyes widened in amazement as Stephanie's foot inched into her lap and wedged her thighs apart. *Boy, these long legs have their advantages. And she's very talented.* Stephanie's big toe accurately zeroed in on its target and moved in sure wide circles.

The hammering in Freddie's head told her that she might indeed come, right here in this restaurant. She could feel her hips rocking slightly to match Stephanie's rhythm. Stephanie discreetly ran her tongue around her lips and smirked at Freddie. Except for the occasional twisted smile, Stephanie looked like someone minding her own business across the table from a friend at dinner. Freddie was so nearly out of control that she had to fight to keep her head from bobbing around on her shoulders.

"Read any good books lately?" Stephanie teased her. Her release was a silent thud. Stephanie deftly drew her foot back to her side of the table. "Darn, I seemed to have stepped in something wet," she whispered. Sue and Nicki shuffled back over to the table before Freddie could respond.

After the toe job, Freddie kept her legs clamped together, sure the slightest movement would yield a loud sloshing noise. Practically over-compensating for her mood earlier in the evening, she made every attempt to be a model dinner companion.

Sue and Nicki did most of the talking. Freddie chuckled, nodded, and made supportive comments where appropriate. If anything, Stephanie was the quiet one throughout dinner. A few times Freddie searched Stephanie's eyes, but the scant lighting made her expressions indiscernible.

Nicki and Sue ordered coffee with liqueur and lingered over the dessert menu. Freddie's legendary appetite had all but disappeared. More than half of her meal was in a take-home box. Had the decision been hers, they would have left forty-five minutes earlier.

Nicki finally looked up from the dessert menu and noticed that Stephanie and Freddie had theirs closed and were looking at each other. She closed her menu and said, "Maybe we're keeping the newlyweds out too late. Let's skip dessert, honey. The coffee should be here any second."

Had they chosen to be virtuous, one of them would have insisted that Sue and Nicki enjoy a leisurely slice of cake after the meal, but neither Freddie nor Stephanie chose the high road.

Forty minutes later, they were walking back into Stephanie's place after dropping Sue and Nicki at the King Kam. The room swap had been somewhat of a drain on Freddie. She just wanted to give the key to Sue, but Sue needed to be officially listed in order to give the number to her answering service. Freddie was sure that the clerk was in on the secret. A redhead with very short hair, she eyed Freddie's bevy of butch beauties with keen interest. Were Stephanie to follow Nicki's suggestion and network in the Kona area, it was quite possible that Donna at the front desk could make some introductions.

They turned on lights, closed shutters, and tended to Pepper at an easy compatible pace as if they'd come home together a thousand times before.

"How do you feel about walking outside naked?"

"What? No foreplay? You always get right to the point, don't you?"

"Hey. I was just wondering if you were feeling shy, in which case I'd bring a basket for our clothes. The hot tub is on the corner of the property. It's fairly secluded, but if the guy down the way has his night goggles on…"

"Every time I think I know exactly what you mean or what you're thinking, you surprise me, Stephanie."

"I think you've had me pretty well figured out from the beginning." She kneeled in front of Freddie and began undressing her. She kissed patches of skin as they became exposed. She then removed and dramatically inhaled the scent of her panties, still damp from the restaurant episode.

Freddie shivered. With Stephanie still on her knees, Freddie was the taller one. Freddie bent and undid the top of Stephanie's dress, letting it fall to the floor. Freddie then dropped to her knees and bit Stephanie's nipples through her bra and watched them harden. She unfastened her bra and freed Stephanie's breasts. As she removed Stephanie's underpants, she drawled, "I guess the fancy footwork took its toll on you too, partner!"

"Me? No. You see, after I stepped in something wet, I also sat in something wet. Come on." She took Freddie's hand and they dashed off to the hot tub. Stephanie's breasts jiggled as she moved.

Freddie helped her uncover the tub and they eased themselves in. They both sighed as they sank into the hot water. It was a clear night and the sky was dotted with magnificent stellar patterns. "The stars are pretty nice from over here, too…and I know what stars do to you."

Freddie positioned herself on the lowest ledge. The water was just touching her chin. She sought Stephanie out with her foot. "Until tonight, I didn't know it was possible to give that much pleasure with a toe. I know I am a rank beginner, but please let me try...Professor." She had been waiting to work the Professor angle into the conversation ever since Nicki had blown Stephanie's cover.

"So far, you have been a very fast learner, my child." Stephanie helped by maneuvering herself into position and spreading herself with one hand to allow Freddie clear access to her. Stephanie fondled her own breast with the other hand.

Freddie could do no more than control her foot and keep from letting the water get too high on her own face. "I thought I might be getting in over my head, but this is ridiculous!"

"I can assure you...it means a lot to me." Stephanie's voice had a throaty quality. "Oh, yeah, baby, just like that. Come on. Come on. That's it." It was followed by a series of cries. When she opened her eyes, Freddie was hovering over her with a shit-eating grin on her face.

"If I were double-jointed, I would lift up my foot and blow on it like a proud cowboy on his gun."

Stephanie pulled her toward her, helped her up to the higher ledge, and proceeded to grab her toe and blow on it. Then she began to suck on her toes. And so began another thirty minutes of hot tub sexploits. They emerged with pruny skin and wobbly legs. Clinging to one another, they walked naked and satisfied to the lanai where Stephanie had left the towels.

Changing Gears

FREDDIE DRIED OFF AND CHANGED into a nightshirt. Stephanie busied herself in the kitchen. They met up in the living room where Freddie
was sitting in a chair. Stephanie had a bucket of ice, tongs, an assortment of cold drinks, two glasses and the kitchen timer. She sat in a
chair on the opposite side, with a coffee table between them. Stephanie
fingered the kitchen timer.

Freddie looked at her curiously. She put it down and asked what
Freddie wanted to drink.

Freddie chose sparkling water and Stephanie poured. She fixed
herself a drink and set it in front of her. Stephanie picked up the timer
again. "Will you do me a favor?"

"Sure."

"I've been thinking about this for some time. There's something I
really want us to do together."

The sound of Stephanie's voice made the hairs on Freddie's arm
stand on end. Was this the kinky portion of the program? She swallowed hard. "What?"

Stephanie turned the timer to 45 minutes. "I have never felt this
attracted nor this comfortable with a lover before. The way things
have been going, I didn't think we'd ever discuss anything but erog-
enous zones, unless we had some structure. So, I am proposing a 45-
minute sexual reprieve. You stay on your side of the coffee table and
I'll stay on mine." She lowered her voice and in the humblest tone she
could muster asked, "Will you do me the honor of letting me get to
know you better?"

"I'd be delighted." Freddie felt self-conscious under the gold-flecked gaze of her towel-clad lover. She cleared her throat. "Where shall we start?"

"Up to you."

"Can this be question and answer, or should we be volunteering information?"

Stephanie clucked her tongue and shook her head. "You must have been every teacher's wet dream." *You certainly were mine*, she thought. "So eager to do everything right. I just want us to talk. If a question comes up that one of us doesn't want to answer, I think we can just say so. Does that clarify it for you?"

"Okay," Freddie steeled herself. "I want to know why you have such a thing about educational backgrounds. I assumed that it was some kind of insecurity about your own education, but something tells me that Columbia doesn't hire construction workers, or freelance high school dropouts with cameras, to teach in their photography department."

Is it too early in the game to pass? These were my rules. "Actually, they don't really have a photography department, just a few courses. Okay. Let's do this right. Dr. Shapiro," she saluted Freddie. "Nice to meet you. I'm Stephanie Amalfi, B.A. in Art History from Ohio University, M.F.A. in photography from Indiana University. Then I was an associate professor at Columbia, where I put in twenty-two credits toward a," She cleared her throat loudly and then lowered her voice dramatically, "Ph.D. in art history."

"How come you didn't mention any of this to me?"

"Ah. Excuse me, darling, let me take my tongue off your clit and tell you about my TA fellowship at Columbia. Very competitive, you know…Ooh, baby, yes, do that again, yes, by the way, did I mention I dropped out of a Ph.D. program? I think I'm coming, oh yes!"

"Cute." Freddie bit her lip to keep from laughing. She wanted to get this all out, and letting Stephanie charm her to distraction seemed counterproductive. "Okay. I just want to know if you have a problem with those of us who slogged through a Ph.D. program."

Stephanie raised her hand. "Look, I knew some very self-important jerks with Ph.D.s back in New York. Sometimes I think people are more concerned with titles and papers than their ability to do anything with them."

"I've met some people like that in academia. I hope I'm not one of them, though."

"I'm sure you aren't. I already told you that I had a bit of a problem with you and Sue being right out there with your titles when I first met you. I guess you're making sure the world knows you are qualified to be writing science textbooks and trading cards with other academics. Sue, for her part, wanted to scare the shit out of me by telling me she was a lawyer, because she thought I was giving you a hard time." Freddie nodded. "And, in case you haven't noticed, I'm a smart aleck. If there's a crack to be made, I tend to go for it. I was thinking that was something we had in common."

"Thanks, I think."

"You know, when I saw Colette, I mean Nicki, it brought back a lot of old memories. It was kind of cool being at Columbia. It had its prestige. There were great facilities."

"What happened? Why'd you...give it up?"

"I was at a crossroads. I was getting paid a modest salary, really modest for someone trying to pay her share of the rent for a loft in Soho. Even with a fellowship and all that stuff, the books alone for the art history course work in the Ph.D. program were costing me a kajillion dollars a semester. I was starting to ask myself if I really wanted to be a perpetual student. And then I got...discovered."

"Discovered?"

"Yeah. Maybe that's an overstatement, but my photographs were in a showing and a private collector offered me some serious money for them. Artsy stuff, black and whites of Central Park at dawn, shots I had set up for my own enjoyment. So my choice was," she leaned forward and lowered her right hand, palm up, "help little Buffy or Chip set up the definitive photograph of the Hudson River for the ten thousandth time, for the usual token salary, or..." She turned her left hand palm up and lowered it, "become a serious photographer making good money." Stephanie sat back in her chair. "In some ways, maybe I sold out. The rest of the faculty was stunned at my decision. A few people who I thought were my friends completely wrote me off."

"Maybe they were jealous."

Stephanie smiled. "Could be. Jill used to tell me to take the Liberace approach and cry all the way to the bank. So, I went from teacher and amateur photographer to professional. I put out a few feelers and I was selling some of my other stuff, working on guidebooks. I wasn't going to give the Rockefellers a run for their money, but I was getting comfortable. And I was happy about it all. The sheer variety of the work excited me incredibly."

The tone of voice and the level of disclosure from Stephanie made Freddie feel warm all over. "Loving what you do is a wonderful gift that many people never get. You can't really believe that you sold out. You're doing what you want to do. That's great."

"Is that what you really think, or are you trying to get on my good side?" Stephanie asked with a wicked grin.

"Don't start. I haven't heard the timer go off."

"Goodie two-shoes."

"Are we having a serious discussion here, or what?"

"Sorry."

Freddie sat up straighter. "The teaching profession loses a lot of people to higher-paying jobs. The U.S. government spends so much money to do studies to try to find out what's wrong with our system and it never dawns on anybody that if they paid teachers better, they could attract more talent and extract more from those people already in the system. Why would someone who could retire at thirty-five from a high-paying job in the computer field want to become a computer science teacher?"

"Uh-oh. I think my cynicism is rubbing off on you."

"No. I see burnout in progress every day at school. A lot of people fall into teaching. Maybe they couldn't get into law school or medical school or they think it's an easy route, lots of time off. On the other hand, some people are really excited about teaching. They wake up in the morning eager to go to class and educate."

"Like you?"

"Like me, on a good day. I think about this stuff all the time, though. I guess if we had a more socialistic society, the computer expert would spend some time as a programmer and some time as a teacher and not have to worry about eking out a decent life. That was one of my favorite things about living in Japan. We were in a private school and we were paid exceptionally well, but we met public teachers and their salaries were not bad, either. They were more or less on a par with people the same age who were working for big companies."

"I can't complain that much about the university. We were certainly better compensated than secondary teachers. It wasn't just about money or even about teaching, for that matter. I still do adult ed courses. In the fall, I'll be teaching at the university branch here. I had a chance to do something more fun that paid better and I jumped at it. To be honest, my main problem was the politics at the university. You may have a hard time believing this, but I'm not the world's greatest ass-kisser."

They both laughed. "Maybe you need more practice," Freddie offered.

The timer beeped.

"Okay, a deal is a deal," said Stephanie. "No more open heart surgery tonight."

"No. Let's not stop. I want to hear everything. I want to know your favorite color and your mother's maiden name..."

"Blue and Frankel," Stephanie offered quickly. She stood up.

"Halt. I'm serious. Let's talk. Just a little while longer." Stephanie smirked and sat back down obediently.

They talked for two more hours. Stephanie told Freddie about the project that first brought her to Hawaii. Freddie told Stephanie about her childhood on Long Island. Stephanie described her artist father, who divorced her mother when she was five. Freddie told Stephanie more about her marriages.

"I know the current charmer's name is Steve. What was number one's name?"

"Shlomo Avraham."

"For real?"

"His English birth certificate said 'Stephen,' with a 'ph,' not to be confused with my soon-to-be ex-husband who spells it with a 'v.' Actually, the English version of his name is Stephen Alan. I called him 'Avi.' He spent a year in Israel in college and he didn't like being called 'Shlomo,' so he became 'Avi.' It's a nickname for 'Avraham,' which is..."

"Abraham. I know. That was my grandfather's name."

"Anyhow, so he settled on 'Avi,' and that's what everyone but his family called him. He found religion when he was a teenager. He was active in Jewish youth groups. His mom always called him 'Stevie.' He hated it. He had checked out the origin of his name and never wanted to use it again. It means 'crown' or 'wealth.' Stephen was the original Christian martyr. And..." She could feel Stephanie grinning at her.

"Hello-o. Don't you think I know that, honey? Remember my name?"

"Oh, shit…sorry."

Stephanie began singing alternate words to "I'm Henry VIII, I Am." "Never was a Willie or a Sam, I'm her third old squeeze, I'm Stephanie…Stéphan the third am I."

Freddie broke into peals of laughter. Tears streamed down her cheeks. When she finally spoke, she said, "I hadn't realized that I had such a predictable pattern." She composed herself a bit. "Do you have any idea what the origin of Winifred is?"

"No, but I bet you're going to tell me."

"It's Welsh and it means 'reconciled, blessed.'"

"That's nice."

"Winifred was a martyred Welsh princess, referred to as the 'patron saint of virgins.'"

It was Stephanie's turn to lose it. She laughed so hard her towel completely unraveled around her. Not only had she deflowered a dyke-virgin, but the patron saint of them, no less.

Freddie took in the view. She had always wanted to be taller, have bigger breasts. She liked looking at Stephanie's body. Her hips were very round, her pubic hair much darker than the hair on her head, her breasts pear-shaped. She thought back to how they had bounced when they'd run to the hot tub. She felt torn. They could talk later, couldn't they? she debated. Well, they could do other things later, too. She chose not to break the spell.

Stephanie felt Freddie's eyes on her body and made no attempt to cover herself up again. She sat still, leaving the next move to Freddie.

"Didn't you ask me to remind you to tell me something later?"

Ow. Stephanie suddenly felt vulnerable. She crossed her arms over her breasts, took in a breath, and refused to make direct eye contact. "I wanted to thank you for…choosing me to…" It was impossible to complete the sentence. *To have this little fling with? To change your life forever?*

"No. Thank you, Steph. For being so giving, so loving, so understanding."

Damn. If only she hadn't added 'understanding.' Where do we go from here, Freddie? When are you leaving me? I know you like my body, but what about the rest of me? Tread softly, Amalfi; don't screw this up. "How are things going in the self-doubt department?"

"I still have a few niggling doubts, but I'm fortified by your strength, your power."

That was a good one. Could I possibly be any weaker or more out on a limb? No, Freddie, you have all the power. Stephanie could feel tears starting to form at the corners of her eyes. "I'm not that strong Freddie, look…" She needed a moment to compose herself. "Why don't you go and get that present that Col—Nicki brought? I think it's still on the lanai."

Freddie stood and went to fetch the box. Stephanie used the towel to dry her eyes. She pulled her knees up and hugged them to her chest. When Freddie re-entered the room, she let her knees drop.

Freddie eyed her in amusement. "If I didn't know better, I'd say you were coming on to me."

"Well, the timer did go off hours ago."

"Ah, the official start of beaver hunting season." Freddie tried to remove the ribbon and wrapping paper from the present. Her fingers were trembling. When she looked up, Stephanie was licking her lips. "Looks like the hunter is about to get lucky," Freddie gasped.

Stephanie crooked her finger at Freddie. "Come here and bring that box with you."

When Freddie was close enough, Stephanie pulled her onto her lap, box and all. She put both arms around her and snapped the ribbon off the present. "My hero," said Freddie.

Stephanie trailed a series of love bites down Freddie's shoulder. Freddie had her hands on the side of the box. "You remember they said there was a curse on this box, don't you?"

"Uhmm. It sounded like they were saying if you opened it, you'd be stuck with me," Stephanie said. She stuck her tongue in Freddie's ear and wiggled it around. Then she whispered, "If I'm too much of a liability, there's a garbage can over there."

Freddie slowly lifted the top off the box. There were two pairs of edible underwear, a bottle of edible massage oil, a copy of *The Joy of Lesbian Sex*, and a small battery-operated vibrator with an extra set of batteries.

Stephanie let out a soft whistle. "Nice haul. If you decide to blow me off, you can still use the stuff. Lots of do-it-yourself possibilities."

"I'd have to be built like Pepper to use the underwear! And don't worry, I've already decided to blow you off…like you've never been blown off before."

It was Stephanie's turn to shudder. "I think the underwear would barely fit on one knee for me, so why don't you model it?"

"Now?"

"Right now. This looks like fun, too," she said, taking the vibrator out of its package and checking that the original batteries worked. "I'll turn off the lights and close things up out here. Rinse this off and meet me in bed." She looked at an imaginary watch. Let's say...in thirty seconds."

"Roger."

After she had used the vibrator and a variety of other moves to make Stephanie howl, Freddie sat on the edge of the bed to catch her breath. She was so sticky she thought the edible underwear would surely disintegrate on its own.

Stephanie pulled her back down and began to lick and kiss the bikini line on the edible panties. She nuzzled and licked at Freddie's backside. "You were right. I need more practice kissing up."

Freddie giggled from the sensation. "What does it taste like?"

"Peppermint cotton candy." She slid up and gave her a big kiss, sharing the flavor, and then went back to work.

It was sweet torture. Stephanie kissed and licked her so slowly that Freddie thought she would die of frustration before her lover put out the growing fire in her. The quickly melting underwear provided an extra touch of friction. Freddie came in rapid thrusts ending in long and loud laughter.

Stephanie held her afterward, stroking her hair. They fell asleep in the embrace, each woman silently wishing that she could freeze time and not have to wake up to face various complications and realities.

Dream a Little Dream of Me

FREDDIE WAS WALKING AHEAD OF *her in the grocery store. Stephanie was piling food into the basket. She was madly putting boxes, cans and packages in the cart—the family size of everything. Freddie turned around. She strained to hear what Freddie was saying. "Oh, Steph. Don't buy that much."*

"Why not?"

"You know."

"No, I don't. Tell me."

"I'm leaving tomorrow."

"Tomorrow?"

"Tomorrow, tomorrow…"

Stephanie woke up with her heart in her throat. Freddie was breathing evenly next to her. Stephanie curled up on her side facing the other way. *Please God, I don't ask for much. Don't I always roll with the punches? Please don't take her away from me. Please.*

The clock on the night table read 4:30. They had barely been asleep two hours, but Stephanie's pain was keeping her wide awake.

She and Stephanie were making love. Stephanie was shouting, "Like that, like that!" She looked up and Steve was standing in the doorway watching her.

She rushed to close the door, but couldn't. He stuck his foot in the way. He looked over at Stephanie naked on the bed. "All right, Freddie. You've had your perverse little affair, now you're coming home." He pulled her arm.

"No. No. Let go of me. No!"

It was contagious. Freddie was crying in her sleep, "No. No.

Let go of me. No!" Stephanie sat up and gathered Freddie into her arms.

"Shh. It's okay, Freddie, it was just a bad dream."

"Steph?"

"Yeah."

"Okay."

"Okay, Freddie."

Freddie fell back to sleep in Stephanie's arms, snoring softly. "It's okay, Freddie," Stephanie continued to chant. *Were you talking to me? I'm not sure I can let go of you.*

Stephanie maneuvered Freddie's head onto a pillow and snuggled up next to her. She tried not to think about the dream or her fears. She recalled the feeling of Freddie in her mouth. She fell asleep with a smile on her face and didn't awake again for four and a half hours.

Falling Deeper

THERE WAS A NOISE IN the distance. Pepper was barking and scratching. Stephanie threw on a robe and headed toward the door. The bell sounded again.

"Coming."

She signed for the FedEx envelope and closed the door. She tiptoed into the bedroom; Freddie had slept through the delivery. She managed to wash her face and brush her teeth and get back to the living room without disturbing her.

Stephanie sat in the living room and opened the envelope, sent from Honolulu the previous day. There was a note from Allison saying that they wanted to use six additional shots, which would increase her payment. That was good. They wanted her to make sure that the crop marks didn't cut out any detail that would interfere with the artistic integrity of the work. She was to compare the original photographs with the cropped version. If it didn't work, Allison wanted her to fix it.

As she spilled the contents onto the coffee table, she was surprised to find that Allison had included a protractor and drafting paper. *What does she think this is, Molokai? She thinks I can't get supplies here, so she needs to include them?*

She dialed Allison on the kitchen phone to tell her the package had come. Allison thanked her in advance and reminded her that, as usual, the deadline was the day before yesterday. "You know, honey, I'd consider installing a flush toilet and buying a refrigerator, if you want me to come visit one day," Stephanie said.

Honey? Who's she talking to? Freddie was listening from the living area.

"Yeah. I bet that's what you say to all your girlfriends. Thanks for the goodies. I'll get it done ASAP. ...Okay. Yeah. I know. Me, too. Bye."

Me, too? Freddie felt her chest tighten. Stephanie walked into the living area.

She turned and saw Freddie standing in the middle of the living room. She had her hair pulled up off her face and there were damp spots around the hairline. "You're up!"

"Uh-huh. Talking to the other woman?" She tried to sound light, but the intonation made the question sound more like *Talking to the other woman, you asshole?*

Stephanie looked her over and chose the more-flies-with-honey approach. "You're so cute when you're jealous."

"I'm not jealous," she muttered, without conviction.

"Oh, no? I haven't seen this particular shade of green—what would you scientific types call it? Algae green? Since last night when you found out that Colette had the hots for me when she was in college."

Freddie had imagined that she'd gotten away with that little silent hissy fit. She looked up at her. The flecks in Stephanie's eyes were like flashing yellow warning lights. The only legal move was to yield. Freddie inched towards her, her mouth in a pout. Stephanie squeezed Freddie against her chest. Freddie could feel tears pushing at the corners of her eyes. Everything about this woman made her feel some sort of strong, overwhelming emotion.

She needed to pull herself together. Strong offense, strong offense. "You were jealous when you saw me with Sue," Freddie said, her voice muffled by Stephanie's robe.

Stephanie kissed the top of her head. "Oh, you mean when I saw the two of you at the airport and I wanted to rip her throat out? Or when she stood in my doorway and I wanted to shove that stupid business card up her ass?"

"Take your pick."

"So? What's your point?" Now she could feel Freddie chuckling against her. Just a second earlier, she thought that Freddie might be crying. She hugged her even harder. *You have no reason to be jealous. I can't imagine feeling this way about another human being.*

They stood in the living room embracing for a long time. Stephanie was making another speech to Freddie in her mind, sending her a silent message. *This is where you belong. I know it and you know it. This jealousy stuff—do you know what it means? It means you want me all to yourself, Freddie. Doesn't that tell you how much you care? And god do I want you. Physically, intellectually, spiritually.*

Freddie backed away a few millimeters. "Steph?"

"Yeah?" *Maybe I was squeezing her too hard.*

"I'm sorry about being such a jerk."

"You already pointed out that it takes one to know one."

"I feel like I've known you all my life," Freddie blurted out. *Oops. Too much.* This was more than being naked. This was like being naked with your skin turned inside out.

Maybe my message got through. "Me, too, baby. Me, too." Stephanie was quick to respond. "You know you can trust me."

"Yeah. It was what's-her-name at the other end of the phone I wasn't trusting."

"Allison is the editor on a guidebook I've been shooting. Yes, she's a dyke, and no, not even an ounce of chemistry. I was teasing her. She's a real snob about life in Honolulu. I think you could get her to Butte, Montana quicker than she'd come to Kona. It's a running joke between us." *Maybe you and I will have our own private jokes one day. I can wait…but tomorrow would be good.*

ᕕ   ᕕ   ᕕ

Stephanie put a plate with half a sunrise papaya and a key lime wedge on it in front of Freddie. Freddie dug in with gusto.

"Mind if I ask a question?" Stephanie began. "I've seen how you are when you suspect a reason to be jealous. This thing with Stevie 2, when you caught him with his secretary. You didn't, like, knock him off, stuff him in a trunk and flee to Hawaii, did you?"

Freddie was searching for a smart answer. The playful expression on Stephanie's face was totally disarming. She finally found one: "Would that make you my moll?"

"I could take the photographs for the tabloids, maybe even write the text myself. Let's see: 'Scorned Wife Escapes to Hawaiian Love Nest… Winifred Shapiro, suspected of murdering her husband, Steven, after finding him in a compromising position with his secretary, Jane P. Slut, was discovered hiding out on the remote Island of Hawaii near the southernmost point in the United States. Since arriving on the island, she is reputed to have become involved with notorious lesbian-at-large Stephanie Amalfi. Rumor has it that the lovebirds have gone into hiding and have not been heard of since this National Investigator exclusive photograph was taken late at night of the two of them making love on top of a car.'"

Before Stephanie had uttered a third of it, Freddie was in stitches. She was holding her sides in laughter-induced pain by the time Stephanie finished.

They ate granola and held hands for the rest of breakfast. As they stood and cleared the table, Freddie said, "I didn't get jealous. I barely flinched. I was pissed. I was so busy working day and night to bankroll his business that I hadn't even noticed we were rarely sleeping together."

They were standing in the kitchen when Freddie went on, "His secretary didn't have a line or wrinkle on her. I mean, why drive a broken down old jalopy when you can have a shiny new sports car?"

"If he saw you that way, he is in dire need of an eye examination."

"No. I saw me that way. He used to be a mild-mannered history teacher. He lived with Mommy and Daddy until he was 31. I have a Ph.D. in biology and a successful textbook series. He has an M.A. in history and he gave up a tenured job to do the stint in Japan. When we got back, the school system wasn't hiring, but there was quite a nest egg in our savings account. That, coupled with a good chunk of my recent royalty checks, put him in the business world…"

"Why don't we go back in the living room and sit for a few minutes?"

"I don't want to bore you with all this crap," Freddie said. Stephanie led her to the sofa. Unlike the evening before, they sat on the same side of the coffee table.

"I'm not bored. Okay, so he started this business with mostly your cash."

"Yeah. He and three friends run a computer research company. It's quite successful. But, can he be conservative and put his share back in the bank? No. He has to have a Porsche and a personal trainer. He used to be this quiet little guy with long hair and a pocket protector. He'd come home with chalk on his pants. Now, he suddenly has a salon cut and three-piece suits. No more chalk, just lipstick on the collar that his workhorse wife was too tired to notice."

"Doesn't it feel better to talk about it?" She put her arm around Freddie's shoulders.

"Yes," Freddie breathed. She could feel the heat of Stephanie's body next to her. "You make me feel so safe."

Stephanie extended her other arm to hold Freddie tighter. "What was the dream about, Freddie?"

"Dream?"

"The one that you woke up so upset from in the middle of the night."

"I don't remember. Did I talk? Sometimes I talk in my sleep."

"Yeah you kept saying, 'Let go of me.'"

"I must have been talking to someone else. I'm sure it wasn't about you."

It had been seven hours, a virtual eternity in newlywed time. She kissed Stephanie's neck and ran her tongue along her collarbone. Stephanie reached for her hand and led her back to bed.

Stephanie lay down and drew Freddie up on her chest. Freddie lowered her mouth to hers. Each flick of Freddie's tongue ignited another flame until she was sizzling from head to toe. She held Freddie to her chest and caressed the small of her back.

Freddie kissed her ears and neck and the tops of her breasts, fondling the undersides. When Freddie finally took a taut nipple in her mouth, Stephanie whimpered. She licked the little mound over and over again, tugging at it with her lips. She brought her hand to the other breast and rolled that nipple between her thumb and forefinger.

Stephanie brought her knee up between Freddie's thighs and rocked it against her wet center. Freddie moved her hand down Stephanie's belly, nestled her fingers into the damp curly hairs, and swirled her fingers around Stephanie's swollen clit in a slow, steady rhythm.

Stephanie pushed into Freddie's fingers, rocking her knee against Freddie. They gasped and cried as they moved together. Stephanie pulled back gently and whispered, "I need to have you in my mouth."

"I need to" reverberated in Freddie's head, causing a fluttering in her stomach. Stephanie seemed to be everywhere at once, taking from her and giving to her at the same time. Her release surprised her, manifesting itself in a series of quiet sobs. In an instant, Stephanie was back at the head of the bed smoothing her hair as she attempted to regulate her breathing.

"I…"

"Shh. It's okay. Don't talk. Shh." Stephanie put her arms around Freddie. "I want to tell you something. Just listen." She paused and blew out a breath. "No matter what you decide to do…I love you."

"Oh, Steph…"

"Shh." They held each other for a long time.

When Freddie felt calmer, she brought her lips to Stephanie's and kissed her. Stephanie groaned. "I'd like to finish what I started earlier," Freddie murmured.

Stephanie felt the knots in her stomach untie one by one when she came. She had never wanted anything this badly in her entire life. She refused to let herself think about what was riding on this relationship. The orgasmic after-ripples were just beginning to subside. She felt emotionally drained, and she stole a short catnap.

Freddie left the bed quietly. She poured some chilled water in a glass in the kitchen and looked out the back window. It was a distant view of what she had seen from the hotel. She shuddered. This time, she had paradise and she was hardly alone.

She carried the glass back into the bedroom. Stephanie was propped up on the pillows. Their eyes locked. Freddie noticed a twinkle that seemed to dance from fleck to golden fleck in Stephanie's eyes.

Stephanie tried to sit up higher on the sloshing waterbed and failed. She managed a weak smile. "Oh, kewpie doll, I'm so A.F.O."

Freddie cocked her head like a puppy trying to figure out where a specific noise was coming from. "A.F.O.?"

"If I told you that the A stood for All and the O for Out, would I have to paint you a picture?"

"Maybe." Freddie perched herself on Stephanie's stomach and faced her. She touched the icy glass to one of Stephanie's nipples. Stephanie shrieked. Her nipple ballooned. "I don't think you're A.F.O. You've got a little bit left in you, Kole."

The idea of spending the rest of the day in bed was tempting, but the project for Allison was hanging over her head. "You're an incredible distraction!" Freddie grinned at her. "But I have work to take care of. Why don't you see what your cuz and your cuz-in-law have planned for the day? I'm surprised they haven't called."

"To hell with them."

Perfectly on cue, the phone rang. Stephanie answered it. "Hello. Hi. Hang on." She put her hand over the receiver and said to Freddie, "The Hades Hot Line."

Freddie giggled and took the phone from her. They made arrangements to meet.

Game Plan

THEY WERE SETTLED INTO THEIR seats and had finished ordering. Sitting opposite Sue and Nicki, Freddie felt that she was surely going to be on the witness stand. She took a sip of her water.

Sue studied Freddie's face. She touched one finger to an eyelid. "You know, Freddie, the airlines charge for extra bags like these. At the rate you're going, they'll be down to your waist by the time you're ready to leave. Are you getting any sleep?"

Nicki slapped her hand away. "Leave her alone, Susie. I think she looks happier than I've ever seen her."

"Really? I think she looks more worn out than ever."

"Excuse me, is this a private conversation or can anybody join in?" Freddie interrupted. They both stopped and waited for her to go on. "I'm fine. I'm a little tired. Yes, I'm happier than I've ever been. Stephanie and I just…fit together."

"That's so cool," Nicki chirped.

Yeah, really cool. Glad you approve, Colette. Freddie rolled her head and was relieved to see the server bringing their salads to the table. As they dug in, Freddie spoke. "You know, you guys don't have much time here, so we really need a game plan. What do you want to do?"

"I'd like to go to the beach and maybe on a snorkel cruise," Sue volunteered.

"Yeah. And how about Waimea?" Nicki added. "My guidebook says that there are nice mountain views and the largest working ranch in the United States is up there."

Freddie started to map out a plan for the next day on half of her napkin. Sue and Nicki, like synchronized swimmers, whipped out their date books and copied the information down. Freddie shook her head. "Do you think I'd have written this on a napkin if I knew you were both packing real paper?"

Stopping back at the hotel room for Sue and Nicki to collect bathing suits and sunscreen was another dip into their world. There were two notebook computers plugged in at opposite ends of the table. A stack of file folders was next to the open one and leather volumes and legal pads next to the other one. "Getting a lot of work done?" she asked neither one in particular.

"Yeah, sure," Nicki answered absently, pulling a towel, bikini, and beach bag out of the suitcase. She sat down on the edge of the bed and stuffed the towel and the bikini into the duffel bag with one hand while she saved something on the computer with the other. Freddie gawked in amazement. She mused that if she were that ambidextrous, she'd use the talent for something else.

Sue came in wearing a bathing suit and kneeled down to look for a cover-up. When she found it, she put it on the bed, picked up the phone, and punched in two dozen numbers to call her office on her calling card. She juggled the phone from ear to ear as she dressed and listened to her voice mail simultaneously. Freddie pretended to cough to cancel the laughter that was gurgling in the back of her throat.

They needed to go and pick up fins, snorkels and masks from one of the local rental shops. Maybe they had underwater cellular phones for professional women pretending to be on vacation. Funny how life could change in a few days! Would she even have thought twice about this compulsive, professional behavior a couple of days earlier? Probably not.

The Calm Before the Storm

Why did I wait so long to do this? she thought. *It feels so good.* The cool water and the gentle waves calmed Freddie. Several scribbled filefish with purplish markings were weaving their way around her. She did a quick body dive to get herself a closer view and snap a picture with her waterproof camera. She resurfaced a few seconds later. She noticed reddish-orange slate pencil sea urchins wedged between rocks. She kicked to get over and check them out. She found a handsome specimen of the state fish, the *humuhumunukunukuapua'a*. The posturing and testy attitude told her he was probably guarding eggs. *I know she does this all the time, but I wish Steph were here to see this.*

Freddie rejoined Sue and Nicki who were holding hands and pointing at various interesting-looking fish. Sue had a black string around her neck with a pink plastic valuables holder trailing from the end of it. A sea turtle passed within inches of them. Sue swam off in the same direction as the turtle. Freddie had lectured them about not touching them.

Nicki made the mistake of smiling too broadly at the sight of the turtle and broke the seal on her mask. She ingested a mouthful of seawater in the process and was up at the surface sputtering and trying to get readjusted. Freddie surfaced to help her.

"That was way cool," Nicki bubbled, fumbling with the foggy mask she had removed from her face. Freddie nodded in agreement and dislodged her snorkel from her mouth. She took Nicki's mask from her, spit into it and rubbed saliva around the lens area. Nicki was unable to hide a slight hint of a princess grimace.

Don't they teach future psychologists blank affect anymore? "This is standard snorkeling etiquette, Nicki. Unless, of course, you were planning to get out of the water and go dig the no-fog goop out of my bag." Nicki shook her head and Freddie handed the somewhat cleared mask back to her.

"Thanks." She replaced the equipment and snorkeled off to catch up with Sue. Freddie decided to explore a bit more on her own. There were at least thirty people in the water and a lifeguard in the chair, so she felt safe deviating from the buddy system.

Ironically, the turtle that Sue and Nicki had pursued had reversed direction and was soon swimming with Freddie. Freddie got a shot of the turtle that she was sure would be full frame. The turtle seemed a bit tired. Could those bowl-you-over New York professional types have the same reputation in the turtle world? Freddie wondered. The turtle was obviously heading for a bit of R&R on the ocean floor. Freddie watched with interest, hovering at the surface.

As the turtle began to nestle into the grainy depths, a flounder that had been completely camouflaged by the sandy bottom skittered away like an underwater Frisbee. Various surgeonfish and others gathered around and picked debris and other forms of fish nutrition off of the turtle's shell. Freddie wished she'd had an underwater video camera with her for the show.

Nicki and Freddie were so taken with the water and the sea life at Kahalu'u Park that they would have stayed in far longer than their sunscreen would allow. Sue was the voice of reason. They showered off under the unseasonably freezing park shower and draped themselves in their beach towels. Someone was making leis at a table in the picnic area. Nicki headed off to watch. Sue rescued a soaking wet wad of dollar bills from the so-called waterproof pink case.

"Look at this!" Sue groused. "Stupid thing was choking me the whole time and then the money isn't even dry."

"I don't think you're going to want to put those back into your Gucci wallet! I'll help you spend it." Sue looked up in horror at the thought. Freddie pointed to the refreshment truck and they walked over. Freddie chose a bubble gum flavored shave ice, a local delicacy of crushed ice with sweet syrup poured over it. Sue picked out mango flavored for herself and passion fruit for Nicki.

They sat at a table and enjoyed the treat. Sue kept managing to get the yellowish goop on her nose. It was even funnier when she tried to make serious conversation with her dotted nose bobbing for emphasis. Nicki wiped it once and licked her finger. It happened again and Nicki said to Sue, dabbing at her nose. "This is your last warning. Next time, I kiss it off. To hell with the consequences."

Freddie felt a pang of intense sadness. Even for two outspoken lesbians who did not try to hide their identity, Sue and Nicki had clear boundaries. Thinking back, she realized that they were not very demonstrative in public. Freddie often felt uncomfortable when she saw straight couples kissing passionately or climbing all over each other in public, but what would it be like to feel ill at ease to touch, hug, or kiss someone square on the lips? She had never thought about the plight of the gay minority.

Okay, it was hard to spend a lot of time thinking of the downside of homosexual love when she was writhing in Stephanie's arms. Or when she was lost in Stephanie's eyes. Or when she watched Stephanie hand-feed Pepper because she thought the dog's stomach might be upset. She was sinking deeper and deeper and unable to move. Why had none of the guidebooks warned of the quicksand in Kona?

Freddie checked in with Stephanie. It was only 3:30, but since Stephanie was on schedule with her work, she agreed to meet them at the hotel. They were talking about making the hour drive to Waimea for dinner. It would be a major change of scenery and fulfill Nicki's desire for a mountain view.

"I need you to bring me a change of clothes," Freddie told her.

"Sure."

"The blue dress that I hung in your closet. The beige sandals in the side pouch of the suitcase and the powder blue bra and panties."

"Does it really matter what color underwear?"

"I have a lot of black stuff. The dress is diaphanous and…"

"Okay, okay. I get the picture," Stephanie laughed. *Black undergarments showing through a sheer dress…be still my heart. If I brought the black stuff, accidentally, could I feign color blindness?*

They made plans to rendezvous at the pool bar at 4:45. The "away team" was going to stop and pick up some of Sue's favorite hair mousse and go back to take real showers at the hotel.

Hit the Road, Jack

STEPHANIE CHOSE A TABLE NEAR the pool. She placed the suitbag that held Freddie's clothes over the back of one chair and plopped down in the one next to it. She and the clothes filled two of the four chairs. She was fifteen minutes early, so she looked over the placard and chose a non-alcoholic strawberry daiquiri.

"Hi. What can I get you?"

"I'll have this frozen strawberry daiquiri," she said pointing to the menu.

"You want a virgin?"

"Yes, please." *My second one this week.*

"Whipped cream?"

"Sure, why not?" Maybe Freddie would have ideas for working off the calories later. She closed her eyes and pictured Freddie in bed that morning. Recalling the scene made her shiver.

She heard the drink being placed on her table. She opened her eyes and took a sip, licking some whipped cream off the bottom of the straw.

Two small kids were splashing in the pool in front of her. She wished she'd brought her camera; the view of Kailua Bay from the King Kam was spectacular. Was it always this breathtaking, or was the world looking more beautiful to her these days?

She crossed her legs and leaned back in her chair. Out of the corner of her eye, she noticed a small man in expensive clothes scrutinizing her. She turned her head slightly to be sure that she wasn't jumping to conclusions and he flashed his pearly whites at her. She turned away. *Lord, what's happening to me? I couldn't attract mud on my shoes a few days ago and now I'm the flavor of the month.*

She began drinking more quickly. It chilled her throat to be plowing through the frozen drink. Maybe she was reading too much into the situation. She was afraid to turn around again. She leaned back in her chair as she had before and saw that he was no longer there. She felt a flood of relief.

Once again, Stephanie closed her eyes and relished in various images of Freddie. She saw Freddie standing in that T-shirt serving up stir-fry. She thought of Freddie keeping her nose just above water as she rendered such ecstasy with one determined phalange. She recalled another scene with Freddie, her shoulders caved and her eyebrows knit, her voice filled with cool anger as she detailed dear hubby's numerous exploits.

Stephanie felt for the drink with her eyes still closed. She picked it up and found the straw with her mouth. She opened her eyes and rubbed them. She saw spots. The sun was low and strong.

"Hi there." It was the little man.

"Huh?"

"Mind if I sit down?" He didn't wait for an answer.

"Look, I'm expecting some people."

"I got you another drink," he informed her with a huge smile.

The server placed the drink in front of her. "You really shouldn't have," she responded firmly.

"No trouble."

"No, I mean, you really shouldn't have!" she said pushing the glass away. She couldn't decide which was more unappealing, drinking another sickeningly sweet non-alcoholic cocktail or being in debt to this troll who had invaded her table.

He gave her an amused look. "Staying at the hotel?" His expression had changed to cocksure. Stephanie crooked a finger at him and he leaned forward. She said very softly, close to his ear, "Look, buddy, actually I'm a local and I know several of the managers. I don't remember inviting you to sit at my table, so I suggest you leave now, before I make a scene."

"Hey, I was just being friendly. You were smiling at me just a few minutes ago."

"I was smiling. I wasn't smiling at you," she said evenly. "Are you getting up, or am I calling someone?"

"All right. You don't have to bite my head off." He walked back to his original table. He sat down and flagged down a server. He asked for a slip of paper and a pen. He wrote fast and furiously. He called the server over again in a few minutes and asked her to pass the note to Stephanie. He turned and left before it was delivered.

One of the servers stopped at Stephanie's table. "The man over there," she turned to point him out. "Oh, he isn't there anymore. Anyway, he asked me to give this to you." She took Stephanie's virtually empty glass and moved the other drink toward her.

"Thanks." When she left, Stephanie pushed the drink back to the other end of the table. She read the note with amusement.

Seems I caught you at a bad time. Don't hold it against me! I sense a strong connection between us. Why don't you give me a call after you see your friends?

Steve

Room 335

She thought about tearing it up, but decided it would be a good dinner table story for which she'd use the I'm-just-a-real-sensitive-guy-who-wants-to-get-in-your-pants note as Exhibit A.

Return of the Keystone Kops

THE ELEVATOR STOPPED AT THE third floor. A man got out and Sue got in. The man was smiling to himself. Sue flashed on the man's resemblance to Freddie's husband, Steve. *They say everyone has a twin somewhere.*

Sue spotted Stephanie at a table near the bar. Stephanie noticed her walking over and waved.

"Hi. Freddie said you worked like a maniac all day!"

"I was happy I got through most of what I needed to do."

Sue looked at the cocktail at the far end of the table. "I've noticed the service is a bit uneven in this place, but how do they expect you to drink it if they put it all the way over at the end of the table?"

"It's a long story. I'll tell you at dinner. Let me take Freddie her clothes." She put the suit bag over one arm as she stood to leave. She reached for the check and Sue slapped it out from under her grip.

"I'll sign for it. Go take her the clothes."

"Okay. Thanks."

"What is this, by the way? Maybe *I'll* drink it."

"A virgin strawberry daiquiri."

"Virgin?"

Stephanie held her free hand out. "Please, I've already been through all that in my head. Hold your razor sharp tongue."

"That's no fun. Maybe if someone else held it..."

Stephanie laughed. *She didn't say 'Maybe if Nicki held it.' Whoa. Is she coming on to me, too? Maybe I have some kind of imbalance and I'm radiating hormones. I smell like sex, so everyone wants me. Or perhaps my imagination is getting the better of me.*

Stephanie knocked on the door and Freddie answered. She was wearing her beach cover-up and nothing else. Stephanie leaned into her with a kiss and kicked the door closed behind her. She could hear the shower running in the background. "How long has she been in there?" she whispered.

"She just turned on the water."

"Speaking of turned on..." Her tongue was back in Freddie's mouth. They fell as one jumble of arms and legs on the bed, the site of their very first kiss. With no underclothes to negotiate, Stephanie had her hand in place in two seconds flat. Freddie attempted to protest, but Stephanie silenced her by sucking harder on her tongue. Freddie snorted as Stephanie stroked her hard and fast. She was just shy of blacking out when she felt a series of quick releases.

As they peeled their bodies apart, they heard the water go off and they chuckled. Stephanie had smoothed herself off and moved to the couch-like thing across from the bed. Freddie worked to make the bed look neater. Stephanie told Freddie about the projects she was working on and Nicki emerged from the bathroom a few short minutes later.

﹏ ﹏ ﹏

Steve had left the bar without actually having a drink himself, so he decided to get a soft drink and ice from the vending machine. On his way back to the room, he had seen a woman going into another room. Though he just had gotten a glimpse, he thought she looked like the woman from the bar. He had started towards her, but she was inside in a flash. Had he heard a moan? He sat on his bed thinking about it. Damn. Maybe she was a hooker. He had insulted her with a drink. Maybe she would have wanted to play if he'd taken out his wallet. The little game had made him rock hard. He took out something other than his wallet.

﹏ ﹏ ﹏

Nicki went down to the bar to meet Sue. As soon as the door closed behind her, Freddie pounced on Stephanie. "They're waiting for us," Stephanie said weakly as Freddie slipped the muu muu over her head. She kissed the tops of both breasts as she reached behind her to unfasten her bra. "Really, Freddie, this can wait."

"I don't think so. Drop your drawers!"

Stephanie gulped and slid her underpants down her legs. Freddie nudged her back on the couch and threw the pillows down on the floor behind her. Freddie got up on her knees and trailed her tongue from Stephanie's belly on down. "I thought this was going to be a quickie, just do it!" Stephanie commanded. Freddie burrowed her tongue into Stephanie and flicked it around as if she'd been doing it all her life. Stephanie adjusted their positions so that they were on their sides in the classic numerical formation and began to lick Freddie, too. Freddie fought the pleasurable distraction and relentlessly tongued Stephanie until she released her and gave into a staggering orgasm. Freddie hopped off the bed like a gymnast and went to the bathroom to turn on the shower.

Stephanie hobbled into the bathroom after her. She was relieved to see that someone had ordered a large stack of extra towels and face cloths from housekeeping. She gave herself a quick sponge bath while Freddie began to shower, then left the bathroom and closed the door. She dressed carefully in front of the bureau mirror, trying to put her hair back the way it was. She looked in the mirror and noticed the flesh around her lips was swollen as the phone rang. She figured it was Sue or Col—Nicki calling from the bar.

"Hello."

"Freddie?" It didn't sound like Freddie.

"No."

"Is this Freddie Shapiro's room?"

"Yes. She isn't able to come to the phone right now, may I take a message?"

"Who's this?"

"Why don't you tell me who's calling first?" *Asshole.*

"This is her husband."

Figures. "She's in the shower. I'll tell her you called," she said coolly.

"I told you who I was. Who the hell are you?"

"A friend. I'll give her your message." She started to hang up.

"Wait a second!" She waited. "I'm...I'm not at home. Tell her I'll call her in fifteen minutes."

"Right."

He hung up without so much as a thank you. *God, he was self-important. Not unlike the jerk at the bar a few minutes ago.*

Freddie came out of the shower in a towel and took the clothes

Stephanie brought out of the suit bag. Everything was there, no substitutions, no additions. She thought what it would have been like to ask Steve such a favor. He would have brought the wrong colors and shrugged it off, telling her he couldn't find something or he thought what he brought would look better. Well, no matter, he was almost out of her life for good.

Stephanie watched Freddie get dressed. She seemed to be deep in thought as she made several round trips between the bathroom and the bedroom. Was she planning the pages of her new textbook, or maybe pondering life as a happy-go-lucky lesbian? She looked fantastic in the blue dress. It was tasteful, yet pleasingly low cut. It was the first time that Stephanie had seen her wearing lipstick and earrings.

"Are you ready?" Freddie asked.

"Uhmm hmm," Stephanie said, her lips trembling. As they closed the door, the phone started to ring.

"That's probably your husband. He called a few minutes ago and..."

"I have nothing to say to him. He's been calling all week." They continued down the hall to the elevator.

"Which long distance carrier are you using?"

Freddie pushed the button for the elevator. "Is this a joke? Everybody's making jokes about long distance service these days."

"No, for real. It was a great connection, like he was practically next door."

"I think he might have just switched companies. If I ever speak to him again, I'll ask him."

Steve slammed down the phone. Where the hell was she and who was this friend providing the icy answering service? If she just went out, maybe he could find her in the lobby or the parking lot. He scrambled to put his pants back on and tripped on one pant leg, tumbling over and banging one knee. He sat for a minute rubbing his knee. He needed to get some shorts.

He started for the door and returned to the bed to rethink his strategy. This was ridiculous. Freddie was with a friend and had left the room. A friend would fortify her. He had to catch her alone and remind her why she couldn't live without him. He would give her a few hours to lose the friend. He looked at his watch. It was 5:45. He'd wait until 8:00 and try her room again. If there were no answer, he'd comb the restaurant and bars and see if she was still at the hotel.

He'd wait and try getting information or the room number from the night clerk. Maybe he needed to flash some cash. If the stupid hotel wouldn't tell him what room his wife was in, he'd stake out the parking lot and surprise her when she came back. He'd position himself where he could see the lobby doors and the parking lot entrance. He'd find her, he was sure of it.

He turned on the TV. In-room erotic movies. All right. Maybe that brunette from the bar would give him a call when she finished. Did he have any condoms in his shaving kit? Probably. He remembered her sitting near the bar with her eyes closed and smiling, a real fuck-me smile. *Don't worry, honey, I'll take care of you*, he thought. *You haven't lived until you've tasted a Shapiro!*

Four Wahines Go to Waimea

THEY WERE IN STEPHANIE'S HONDA headed north. Freddie had offered the use of the rental car, but Stephanie had declined. She said she liked to drive. She told them that Waimea was also called Kamuela. She pointed out the little port area they passed on the way where a recent Hollywood film had been shot.

Nicki responded to every tidbit of information and occasionally asked questions. Freddie had lost her powers of concentration. She had her hand on Stephanie's thigh and was having pleasant flashbacks to their time together in the hotel room, which caused new waves of excitement to run through her. She tightened her hold on Stephanie's thigh. Stephanie took her right hand off the wheel and covered Freddie's hand with hers.

They pulled up to a restaurant called Merriman's. Stephanie had made reservations and, once again, the restaurant people seemed to know her. They were shown to their table almost immediately, having to gingerly navigate through the people waiting.

"This is one of the original HRC restaurants," Stephanie told them.

"HRC?" Sue asked.

"Sorry. Hawaiian Regional Cuisine. A lot of the vegetables are local and there are local touches added to typical Pacific Rim dishes. In other words, it's like Spago with a Hawaiian accent."

"Everything on the menu looks terrific. What do you recommend?" Nicki asked her.

"It's all great. Let's see...Oh, the Papaya Bisque is listed with the specials. I've seen this recipe in one of the Hawaiian cookbooks and always wanted to try it. I think I'll start with that. The seared ahi Caesar salad is delicious, too."

The restaurant lived up to Stephanie's praise. The food was fabulous, Freddie thought. Everything felt right. Over dinner, Stephanie had regaled them with the story of the guy whom she called the "little prick" at the pool. She pulled out his note and read it dramatically. They had laughed and laughed. Another little prick named Steve, thought Freddie. There was a lot of that going around.

Stephanie was watching Nicki eat the coconut crème brûlée. Nicki was only five or six years younger than she was, but she had the metabolism of a teenager. Nicki fed Sue a spoonful and she sighed in pleasure. With that kind of recommendation, Stephanie and Freddie felt compelled to have a spoonful.

Sue hadn't had anything to drink all night and she'd taken two refills on the Kona coffee, saying that she had some work to do when they got back to the hotel. The other three had split a bottle of wine, so Sue was the logical choice as designated driver.

Settling in back with Freddie's head against her shoulder and her arm around her, Stephanie wondered if she'd ever ridden in the back seat of her own car before. She couldn't think of such an occasion.

Sue dialed in an FM station playing love songs. Stephanie caressed Freddie's neck with her fingers. Nicki and Sue were talking over the radio about some friends who were renting a place in Vermont for the summer. Freddie turned toward her and they kissed softly.

Stephanie was trying to listen to the conversation. She was trying to be well behaved. Every nerve in her body was begging her not to be so adolescent, but Freddie wasn't helping. She had reached purposefully under Stephanie's muu muu. Oh, hell. Stephanie spread her legs wider and slipped her fingers under Freddie's bra. They worked hard to control their breathing and the occasional pant seemed to get lost in the din of the radio and the East Coast-paced conversation in the front seat.

Freddie stuck her fingers in Stephanie's mouth and Stephanie licked them clean. Stephanie then parted the powder blue panties and did some of her best work on Freddie. They held onto one another and let their bodies calm down.

Nicki glanced over into the back seat. "I think the lovebirds have fallen asleep."

Freddie started to giggle but swallowed it back. She then emitted a fake snore, which made Stephanie chuckle noiselessly.

"Isn't that cute?" Nicki continued.

"They do make a cute couple," Sue agreed.

A while later, Stephanie yawned and suggested that they stop at a scenic point. There were stars and moonlight making the ocean visible from the cliff. The two couples held hands and enjoyed the vista.

Before starting the car, Sue turned to Freddie in the back. "When's the last time you talked to Stevie Boy?"

"He called the first night I was here and I hung up on him. He's called several times since. I just threw the messages away. Why?"

"You haven't returned any of those calls?" Sue asked.

"No. Would you have?"

"That's not what I mean. When I was going down to the pool, I saw a guy who looked just like him." Sue turned the key and started the engine.

"That's impossible. He called from home right before we left the hotel. Stephanie took the message."

"Actually, he said he wasn't home," Stephanie contributed.

"I was just thinking about the little prick named Steve who hassled you, Stephanie. That would have been right before I saw you. How long had he been gone at that point?"

"Two minutes?"

"Can you describe him in detail?" Sue asked.

"Not really. I was trying to ignore him. He was about 5'3" with medium brown hair that was expensively styled. His clothes seemed nice. He was wearing a polo shirt and brand name khaki pants. I don't remember much."

"Did his ears seem a little big for his face?" Nicki asked.

Freddie almost defended him through sheer force of habit, but closed her mouth.

"Oh, I just remembered something else. He had a really nice white gold chain around his neck."

"That filthy bastard!" Freddie shrieked. "Let's get back to the hotel. I'm going to put an end to this once and for all!"

"Yeah, step on it, Jeeves," Stephanie teased from the back seat.

Sue gave it some gas and Honda-Honey squealed back onto the highway.

Meanwhile, Back at the Ranch

AT 8:00, STEVE WAS OUTSIDE pacing. He walked back and forth between the parking lot and the front door awning more than a dozen times. The bell captain asked if he could help him. He declined politely and stopped pacing.

Finally, at 9:15, a red Honda pulled up to the door. Every door opened and a woman emerged from each one. Freddie had been in the back seat. That big brunette from the pool came out the other side of the back seat. He squinted and recognized Freddie's cousin Sue and her girlfriend. What was her name? Vicki, that was it.

Maybe the brunette liked girls, too. Was that her he saw going into that room? Maybe she had a girlfriend at the hotel. Or were Sue or Vicki doing something on the side? Perhaps a threesome. He seemed to remember that Sue and Vicki were into that kind of thing. What was Freddie doing with this motley crew? What a heart on that Freddie, what a bleeding heart.

Well, this just wouldn't do. He couldn't possibly talk some sense into Freddie in this ménage of man-haters. He dashed to the back of the building and came into the lobby from the pool area. He'd lived in L.A. all his life. Some of his friends from the drama club in high school were actual movie personalities. This was his chance.

"Hi." *Big smile to the man at the desk.*

"Hi."

"I can't seem to find my key. My name's Shapiro."

"What's the room number?"

"Damn. I just can't seem to remember it. My wife usually handles stuff. In fact, the room is in her name. She tells me I'd have trouble keeping track of my head if it weren't attached."

"What's your wife's name?"

"Freddie, uh, Winifred."

"Yes, here it is."

"You got some I.D. or somethin'?"

Steve pulled out a California Driver's license.

"Thanks, Mr. Shapiro," the clerk said, and pressed a new card key for Steve. "It's room 341."

"No. Thank you. You're a lifesaver. It drives Freddie crazy when I lose things. Now, she'll never have to know."

The clerk smiled at him. He nodded a thank you and made a beeline for the elevators. As he punched the up button, he looked around for Freddie or any of the others he'd seen by the car. Good. Still no sign of them. As soon as the door opened, he got in and pressed three, followed by the close button. When he got to the third floor, he scurried to Freddie's room and unlocked the door. Was this the room that he'd seen the brunette going into? Naw. That must have been the one next door. This room looked like a mini suite. There were two computers plugged in. Two? Maybe Freddie was letting those two pussy-eaters use her room as an office. He noticed Freddie's Lakers T-shirt that she used for a swim cover-up on the bed.

He sat on the bed and waited. Where the hell was she, already? How long does it take to wave bye-bye to her cousin's buddy? Were they next door talking? He couldn't imagine what was taking this kind of time.

❧   ❧   ❧

"I'm telling you, Freddie, you need a plan," Sue told her.

If she had a nickel for every time Sue started a sentence with "I'm telling you, Freddie," she could have given up her job.

"I'm just going to go to his room and tell him to get his sorry *okole* out of here," Freddie spat.

"*Okole?*"

"That means…"

Sue interrupted Stephanie. "We can figure out what it means."

"I thought that was the name of the airport," Nicki said earnestly.

"That's *Keahole*," Stephanie told her. "Speaking of which, are you getting some sort of kickback from the tourist bureau? You have some family member coming in every day."

"You think this is very amusing, do you?" Freddie snapped at Stephanie.

"Come on, Freddie, you aren't mad at Stephanie. Stay focused. I do think you need to talk to him. And you're going to have to figure out what you want to do as far as lawyers and stuff. As you might remember after the first little prick, divorce is serious business. Kicking his ass out of Kona would just be a stopgap measure," Sue stated.

"I want to talk to him, all right. I want to find out what the hell he wants from me. I told him I'd set him free. He can pick up all the sexy numbers at all the pool bars in all the universe. Coming on to my Steph, though, that's the last goddamn straw."

Stephanie had a million little jokes about this newly exposed butchly protective side of Freddie, but tears were streaming down Freddie's face. Stephanie felt around in her bag for some tissues and mopped at Freddie's eyes. They were silent for a few seconds. Another car wanting to unload in front of the hotel spun them into action.

Stephanie shot a just-a-minute wave to the driver behind her. She retrieved the keys from Sue and walked over to the driver's side. She told everyone to get in. She drove them over to the parking lot and parked in one of the side spaces along the building.

"This is the plan," Sue started. "You go in there and talk to him, but not one drop of emotion. Don't give him any more credence, affection or sympathy than you would the patio furniture. Got it?"

"Got it. Let me see that note, Steph, it has his room number on it." Stephanie pulled the crumpled note out of a pocket and gave it to her.

Sue opened her purse. "I want you to take my pocket tape recorder. Just leave it on in your bag; it will pick up everything. Tell him what you want to say and get out of there. If it takes more than 10 minutes, we'll send the cavalry," Sue promised.

When they got into the lobby, Freddie asked, "How red do my eyes look?"

"You look fine, Freddie," they all mumbled at once. Freddie looked at them pleadingly.

"You don't look like you've been crying, baby. You look like you are going to put a slick little bastard in his place. Hang tough," Stephanie told her.

Something about the room smelled very feminine and sexy to him. Although it had been months and months since they'd had sex, he always thought that part of their relationship was nice. Freddie wasn't demanding and always told him he was good—especially if he asked her once or twice. So far, they weren't divorced. It wasn't even a legal separation. Maybe it was time he demanded his husbandly rights.

He stripped to his maroon Calvin Kleins. He turned off the light. He got under the covers and waited for her. As he recalled, she had looked pretty foxy when she stepped out the car.

The others stopped in front of room 341 and let Freddie walk past them to Steve's room. She knocked and Sue gave her the thumbs up sign. Nicki put the card key in their door and pushed it open.

"Surprise!" Steve shouted throwing the covers off. The tight briefs only served to accentuate the flagpole effect.

"Right back at you, slimeball," Sue shouted back.

"I didn't know it was going to be a party! Is this for girls only?" he asked. He chose the politically incorrect term expressly to irritate Sue. "Your girlfriend and I already started playing, a couple of hours ago," he said, leering at Stephanie.

"Listen, you scummy excuse for a person," Stephanie began.

"I don't think you've called him enough names. You left out dickhead, animal, bastard..." Sue joined in.

"Hey. Is this our foreplay?" Steve asked. All three were essentially talking at the same time. Nicki just stood there with her mouth wide open.

"Enough," Freddie screeched from behind. The door was partially open and it would have been extremely entertaining for anyone happening to walk by at the moment.

"What are you staring at, Vicki?" Steve shot at Nicki.

"It's Nicki!" the others shouted in unison.

Freddie had pushed through them and stood and regarded him, arms akimbo. She kicked his pants up to him from the floor. "Get these on and get back to your room. I want to talk to you. Everybody already knows how stupid you are, so you better not open your filthy little mouth until we leave this room."

Steve gathered up his clothes and managed to hop into his pants despite his physical state. Freddie's tough talk had only served to excite him further. Freddie headed down the hall before he had his pants zipped. Sue held the door open for him and ushered him out in a grand sweeping motion. He could hear muffled laughter when that door shut behind him.

Freddie didn't turn around at all. When she reached his room, she stood in front of the door waiting for him. The distance to his room seemed to have lengthened. Didn't Freddie have any idea how hard it was for a man to walk in this condition? He pulled his own card key out of a pocket and inserted it into the door.

When they were both inside, he touched her shoulder gently. She shrugged his hand away and sat down in a chair at the far end of the room.

"Freddie, I didn't mean to embarrass you. I thought you'd be alone. I wanted to surprise you. I just wanted us to be together. Can't you believe that?"

No, not at all. "Steve, which part of 'I never want to see you again as long as I live' did you not understand?"

"Come on, Freddie. We're good together. You're the only woman I care about. You know that." He started again, trying to sound somber. "It's been kind of a mid-life crisis for me, baby."

"Don't call me that." *Only Steph can call me that.*

"I know you're mad. And I know I'm weak. But...I can change."

"Like today at the pool?"

"What? You really think there was anything between me and that...that...Amazon bitch?"

She wanted to slap him, but that would have involved touching his skin. Instead she held the crumpled note out at arm's length and waved it. He had the decency to lower his eyes. "Why are you here, Steve?"

"I want us to talk."

"There's nothing to talk about. It's over, finished, done, gone, finito—let me know when I hit a word you'd truly understand."

Steve was quiet for a few seconds.

"What difference does it make that I had an affair? We hadn't done it in months. I thought you were relieved. I never thought you were that into sex anyway."

Freddie laughed. How many times had she had sex this week? She was losing count. "You're right, Steve. I was never very into sex with you." She laughed again. She could see his face cloud in anger and she could have worked up to a real belly laugh, given the opportunity.

He looked at her. Something about her appeared totally different. Was it a little sun? Her face looked less washed out than usual. She was in control, enviably in control. *Was this a slam about his performance in the sack?* Nobody else had complained. "Didn't we have some good times?" he asked, insecurity gnawing at his vocal cords.

"Sure. That was then and this is now."

"What does that mean?"

"It means I want more from my life these days. I'm going ahead with the divorce proceedings. As per the pre-nuptial agreement, you will have no claim on my royalties or anything purchased with that money, including my share of your company. Here's some free advice. Sell the Porsche and start putting some of your earnings and company dividends away. The cash cow is moving on to greener pastures."

He stood and attempted a boyish smile. "I can't believe you think this is about money. I love you and I miss you. Love is different than sex. I love you and only you."

"I'm sorry, Steve. I'm not buying it."

"Who are you and what have you done with Freddie? 'Not buying it' and that 'cash cow' bit, I bet you've been rehearsing that with your lesbo cousin. It doesn't sound like you at all. You planning to parade her in with some legal mumbo jumbo for extra emphasis?"

Everything about him was making her skin crawl. "What you've proven by coming all the way to Hawaii is that in addition to being a liar, a cheat and an all-around jerk, you're a homophobe to boot."

"I'm sorry. I'm not trying to be a jerk. I'm just feeling emotional. I call you a dozen times and you don't return my calls. I just wanted to talk to my wife. You're still my wife, Freddie. I need you."

Freddie just looked at him. She was tired of going around in circles. He didn't need her; he needed her money. "I think we've said all there is to say, Steve."

"Give me one more chance. I'll do anything you want. I'll never so much as look at another woman again."

Sorry, you little jerk, but I don't think I could make that promise. "It's too late. I've met someone and it's serious."

❦   ❦   ❦

A few doors down, Stephanie was pacing in the other hotel room. Nicki was frantically typing away at her computer. Sue grabbed Stephanie's arm. "Sit down. You're wearing a hole in the carpet."

"Tell me something, Sue, does he stand a chance of winning her back?"

"In this universe? I don't think so. This is about money. He's more interested in her adoptions than anything else."

Adoptions? Were there kids involved? Stephanie looked blankly at Sue.

"Adoptions. Textbook adoptions. Most of the high schools in Florida, Texas, New York and California are using her materials. That's a lot of books. She's very successful, you know. "

"She hasn't said much about that."

"You see," Sue went on, "she was more than halfway through her research for the first edition of her textbook when they got married. I made sure she had him sign a pre-nuptial agreement stating that he had no claim on revenue from her royalties."

"Can I ask why, in this day and age, she uses his name?"

"I think it was a combination of things. She hated her maiden name, Berkowitz, so she had never really lost her first married name. She might have even kept that, but they actually thought she might be pregnant when they got married. Steve convinced her that she should have the same last name as Junior. It turned out that she was suffering from amenorrhea due to stress. I think she got her period during the honeymoon."

Stephanie was quiet. The thought of Freddie almost having a child with that conceited little elf was completely disturbing. "If she signed a pre-nup, doesn't that mean that he's out of luck?"

"Exactly. That's why he's over there telling her how much he adores her and can't live without her. Her money pays for all the little extras—his manicures, new tires for his Porsche. He's gotten worse instead of better. He went from being a little geeky social studies teacher to an entrepreneur. He's drunk with power and his wife has been his support. As far as he's concerned, she's an ATM with boobs."

"Yuk! I'm trying to work, Susie. If you're going to distract me, couldn't you guys talk about something else besides that little jerk?"

🙖 🙖 🙖

Down the hall, Steve was trying to digest Freddie's statement: "You've met someone and it's serious?" He decided it was his turn to laugh. "Who, the porter?" Snicker. "The bartender at the pool?"

She grabbed his collar. He stopped laughing. "Steve," she growled, "this conversation is over. You had a chance to be part of this trip with me and you blew it. I don't want to see you again. I'll speak to my lawyer in the morning and make everything official. Have a nice time. Don't eat too much poi, I hear it can be constipating." She smiled pleasantly and walked out the door.

Later, in 341, the group listening to the conversation on Sue's mini tape recorder requested that Freddie's exit line be repeated three times, laughing harder each time.

They discussed the plans for the next few days. Sue and Nicki lamented that they only had two more days on the island. They wanted to go on a snorkel trip and to sponsor a big party to celebrate Freddie's freedom. They talked excitedly about various plans. Stephanie and Freddie didn't head back up the hill until 1:00 a.m.

What About Us?

THERE WAS AN EASY SILENCE between Stephanie and Freddie on the way back to the house. Freddie was resting against Stephanie as she drove. Stephanie kept telling herself to leave well enough alone. She knew that she'd won the battle, but when would she know whether or not she'd won the war? This was certainly not the time to be asking Freddie for a status report on their relationship. Stephanie was expected to be understanding and sensitive, everything the husband was not.

When they got into the house, they hugged for a few minutes. Freddie was silently thanking Stephanie for being there for her and Stephanie was praying that this was still the beginning and not the end.

Stephanie took care of Pepper while Freddie started to get ready for bed. When Stephanie joined her in the bedroom, Freddie smiled at her. Freddie was wearing a black negligee. Stephanie did a double take, and her heart started slamming against her chest. She was beginning to understand the idea behind "What doesn't kill you makes you stronger."

When she finally found her voice, she said, "I didn't know we were dressing for bed tonight, my peignoir is at the cleaners."

"In that case, you'll have to come to bed naked. I believe those are the rules," Freddie told her.

Stephanie made a quick trip to the bathroom to wash her face and brush her teeth. Were they just using torrid sex to avoid discussing the issues at hand? She wasn't a kid anymore, could she survive all this sex? If it was time to go, though, a heart attack from the big O wasn't a bad way to kick the bucket.

When she returned to the bedroom, Freddie was sitting on the edge of the bed. She smiled broadly and her eyes smoked with a come-hither expression. Stephanie bent down and kissed Freddie ever so gently. Freddie pulled her down so they were side by side facing one another. Stephanie's legs hung over the end of the bed.

Stephanie's hand went to Freddie's shoulder to lower one side of the negligee. Freddie caught it and held it back. "Slow down, Steph. I want this to be nice and slow."

Her stomach ached. *Was this a good-bye fuck? What are you doing to me, Freddie?* She closed her eyes. *Don't let me cry.*

Freddie kissed her eyelids, the tip of her nose, the side of her face. Stephanie opened her eyes. Their faces were very close together and they looked into one another's eyes. It made her middle-aged eyes ache to look at something at such close range, but she would not be the first to look away, Stephanie thought.

Like the lip synch on an old movie on television, Freddie's lips seemed to move before the words could be heard. "I love you, Stephanie Amalfi."

God, let it be even a quarter as much as I love you. "And I love you, Freddie."

Freddie placed Stephanie's hand on her shoulder and helped her remove a corner of the black gown. Stephanie licked and kissed Freddie's shoulder and left breast over and over again. *Okay, Freddie, we'll take this slow. When I get finished with you, you will be begging me to speed things up.* Freddie sighed and quivered beneath Stephanie's expert tongue.

The renewed security that each felt in the relationship pulsated through every move and was reciprocated in triplicate. Every kiss tasted sweeter, every caress touched a deeper place in each woman's soul.

Telling Dreams

THE LINE BETWEEN THEIR LOVEMAKING and sleep was not well defined. One minute, they were passionately caressing one another and the next they were asleep in each other's arms. Freddie moaned and mumbled.

Steve is sitting at a bar with a drink in front of him. Freddie and Stephanie are at a table close by. Freddie gets up and walks over to him.

"You were right all along, Steve. My friend Stephanie really thinks you're a hunk and a half. She wants you desperately."

"Really?" Pant. Pant.

"Oh, yeah, like you wouldn't believe. Want to see a little thigh? She's got great legs."

"Uh-huh!" Freddie motions to Stephanie and she lifts her muu muu up over one leg to reveal one thigh.

"Wow."

"Nice, huh?" Freddie says to him. "Actually, she's not wearing any underwear. Do you want to see? It's a perfect curly black triangle. Interested in taking a peek?"

"Oh, yes, please." Freddie makes an uncovering motion to Stephanie. Stephanie raises the muu muu in a flash to reveal that she is indeed not wearing underwear.

"What do you think, Steve?"

"You're right. Perfect." Steve's mouth is hanging open and his eyes are wide.

"Okay, here comes the fun part. Do you want to smell her pussy, Steve?"

"Yes, oh yes." He starts to get up off the chair, but Freddie pushes him back.

"Hang on now. Are you sure, Steve? Are you very sure?"

"I'm positive."

"Tell me what you want, Steve. I want to hear you say it."

"I want to smell your friend's pussy."

Freddie looks Steve in the eyes and blows a long stream of air into his face. "There you go, Steve, take a whiff."

Steve turns beet red. Freddie grabs Stephanie's hand and they leave the bar. They are both cackling like two witches on steroids.

"Oh, Freddie, I can't believe he fell for that tired old joke!"

"I told you where his brains are located." They laugh again.

Stephanie awoke with a start. Freddie was laughing in her sleep. How cute! Freddie rolled over and quieted down. Stephanie closed her eyes and fell back to sleep.

"Ms. Amalfi, Ms. Amalfi, could I please trouble you for a short interview?"

"Sorry, I'm not granting interviews at this time. I submitted a press release about my new show. I'd be more than happy to provide your publication with a copy."

"But, Ms. Amalfi, this is not any ordinary magazine. It's Sappho's Home Journal. There'll be a copy of this in every self-respecting lesbian household. At several awards dinners recently, you've thanked your lover for her many contributions to your work."

"Yes, my lover is very inspirational."

"Details, Ms. Amalfi, we want details. Don't give us your press releases; we want to know about your private releases. How has your lover helped your work?"

"In every way imaginable."

"I'm sure you can be more specific than that."

"When I set up a mountain photo, the curves remind me of her fabulous breasts, and what can I say? I'm inspired."

"Better. Keep going."

"When I take animal photos, I recall her writhing around my bed ready to pounce all over me. The shots of tide pools remind me of the flood of moisture that gathers around her when I'm about to go down on her."

"What about your prize hurricane shots?"

"Use your imagination!"

"Your lover after wild, unbridled sex is what you see when you shoot broken branches from trees and houses without rooftops?"

"Something like that."

"Ms. Amalfi, you're a pervert!"

"Sorry, I didn't mean to offend you."

Offend me? Ha! I'm making you the cover story."

Higher and Higher

STEPHANIE SHOT OUT OF BED to a standing position just as the phone rang. Had the ringing jarred her awake? She snatched the portable from its cradle and sank back down on the waterbed. "Hello?"

"Steph, Sue here. How's Freddie doing?"

"Could you hang on?"

Sue sounded as if she had been awake for hours. Stephanie rubbed her eyes vigorously. The clock read 7:56. Where was Freddie, anyway?

"Hi, Sue. I think Freddie's doing better—she calmed down quite a bit after we left the hotel."

"Good. We saw the little weasel at breakfast. He's incurably smug—probably betting she'll change her mind and run back to him."

Stephanie clucked her tongue in response. The events of the night before replayed in her mind in a rush. *Freddie told me she loved me last night.* She and Freddie were turning some corner in their relationship, but Stephanie didn't necessarily want to share that with Sue. A clatter from the kitchen disrupted Stephanie's musings. *Aha.* That was the sound that had jolted her awake.

"I think I hear Freddie in the kitchen. Let me get her for you," Stephanie offered, padding across the room.

"You know, I can tell this to you. Nick and I decided that since we've come all this way, we might as well really see the Islands. We called and changed our plans. We're going to spend five more days here, instead of two. This way, we can get to the volcano and see the gardens over in Hilo, maybe even go up to the to the top of Mauna Kea. Don't worry, we'll rent a car and Freddie doesn't have to babysit us. After that, we're planning two nights at a resort on Maui and the last two in an Oahu hotel."

Instead of going to the kitchen, Stephanie walked around the bedroom in confusion—she was still very groggy and not at all sure where Pepper could have gone. *Maybe it's all the funky dreams that are leaving me so tired.*

Sue countered the silence. "This doesn't have to affect you and Freddie, Steph. We plan to rent our own car. We'd be more than happy to leave you two alone as much as possible. We know what it's like when couples get together…"

"No… Sorry, Sue. For some reason I'm having trouble waking up this morning and my dog seems to be AWOL…Freddie?"

Stephanie peered into the kitchen. Freddie was scrubbing what appeared to be a sinkful of stainless steel bowls. Pepper was curled up on the area rug at Freddie's feet with her eyes closed.

"Morning. I was trying to get a bowl down to mix up some pancake batter and they all fell out. I was going to wipe them off, but they seemed dusty, so I thought I'd just wash them all. I guess it sounded like thunder. Oh, sorry, are you talking to someone on the phone?"

Stephanie shook her head and handed the receiver to Freddie.

Stephanie poured herself a cup of coffee. Was it a hangover? Could the two glasses of wine she had early the evening before have caused her fog? She faded in and out of Freddie's conversation.

"That's great! Oh, wait a minute. It sounds like we have another call. Will you be at the hotel for a few more minutes? We'll call you right back, okay?" Freddie pushed the flash button and handed the phone to Stephanie.

"Hello…hey, how are you? You did?" Wendy had left her a message the night before, but she hadn't even bothered to check the machine. Stephanie opened a kitchen drawer and picked out a wooden spoon and a spatula to hand to Freddie.

"I should have called you guys sooner. I've been so busy…hang on a sec. You need help or anything?" she asked Freddie.

"No. This will take me a while, go talk to your friend." Freddie smiled.

Stephanie sighed. *Freddie told Sue that* **we** *had a phone call. She's making* **us** *breakfast in* **our** *kitchen. Does that mean she's moving in?* Stephanie had so much she ached to ask Freddie, but for the moment, she would leave her to the various domestic activities she was undertaking in the kitchen.

"I'm back," Stephanie announced into the receiver, picking up her coffee mug and walking to the living room. "Man, I have this awful logy feeling this morning. I don't usually have such a problem after two glasses of wine!" She plopped onto the sofa, sighed again and took a long swallow of the coffee.

"I knew it! I told Deb that I had this premonition that things were working out with your kewpie doll!"

"Huh?"

"Alcohol is not the only known cause of a hangover, you know."

"Ah." She felt her face flush. All right then, but she and Freddie had been auditioning for the lesbian sex Olympics for the last few days, why the sudden hangover? She'd even had what amounted to a whole six hours of sleep the night before.

"We're dying to meet her."

"I'd love to introduce you. Maybe we can drive over there."

"It would be more than halfway here for you guys, but when I called last night, I was asking if you wanted to meet us and head up to the top of Mauna Kea. Deb wants to take our new four-wheel-drive SUV out for a spin."

"Damn, you folks got a new car? I don't think I've asked you what's new in your life in ages—just go on and on about my own damn problems. Some friend I am, yeah?"

"We can give you a hard time about that when we see you. So, are you free tomorrow?"

Just as she was about to make plans for them, she remembered the wrinkle and the strong accent that went with it. "Freddie's cousin and her lover are here for the next few days. I'm not sure what they have planned."

"They would be welcome, but you really need four-wheel drive to get up to the summit. I don't think we can all squeeze into the car—it's pretty much a five-passenger vehicle. Of course, a couple of us can hang out at the Visitor Information Station for a few hours and the other four could go up. I'd be more than happy to wait below. I've been up there before, and it's impossible to think clearly when the air is so thin!"

"I'd be glad to stay below, too. As it is, I can't seem to focus the way I used to at ordinary altitudes."

"I see. This may have already occurred to you, but the vibe I'm picking up is that you're in love."

"You psychic types are so perceptive."

~ ~ ~

After a short chat with Freddie and a handful of phone calls, Stephanie arranged for Sue and Nicki to rendezvous with Wendy and Deb in downtown Hilo at 3:00 p.m. They would drive up to the summit for sunset and meet Stephanie and Freddie at the Visitor Information Station at nightfall for hot beverages and stargazing.

Freddie's homemade pancakes turned into a lengthy project, so Stephanie took out the remainder of the photos for Allison's project and spread them out on the dining room table. She had just begun to measure the angles of a shot of a macadamia grove when Freddie came in with a platter of banana pancakes.

"I guess we should eat in the living room or on the lanai," Freddie said. Stephanie motioned toward the lanai and walked in front of her to slide the door.

"Smells heavenly."

Freddie set the platter down on the lanai table and went back to the kitchen for utensils and other paraphernalia. Stephanie looked up at her when she reentered the room.

"I love you, Freddie."

"Maybe you'd better taste them first…"

Stephanie held her gaze and didn't smile at the quip. "Steph…" Freddie practically kneeled in her lap to embrace Stephanie. The pancakes had been her attempt at business as usual. Maybe it was too soon to be domestic and mundane. The ache consumed Freddie. She felt Stephanie's tears on her cheek.

"I just had to tell you in the light of day."

"I love you, too, baby."

"I'm glad. Let's eat. I don't want all that hard work to go to waste."

They sat at the lanai table mostly pushing their food around their plates. Stephanie could feel the coffee helping her return to lucidity, so she accepted another cupful. They didn't speak much, communicating with small noises of appreciation and hand signals.

Freddie finally broke the spell. "This romantic stuff is hell on my appetite. I'm usually a very good eater."

Stephanie chuckled. "I was watching you that night at the Mexican restaurant and wondering where your dinner mate was. If we don't finish all of these, we can toss some into the yard. If the turkeys don't stop by today, the cardinals and finches will go for it."

"Pepper caught a little piece of banana that I dropped in the kitchen. I didn't think dogs cared much for fruit."

"Pepper loves fruit, and the local apple bananas are her favorite!" At the mention of her name, Pepper put her front paws on Stephanie's leg and stretched delicately. "Subtle. That wasn't an invitation to beg, you know."

Stephanie's actions contradicted her words as she speared a small corner of the pancake for the dog. She looked up to see Freddie watching her. "This is the no-begging-at-the-table-unless-I-feel-like-feeding-you policy." Freddie nodded sagely at the clarification.

*   *   *

That afternoon, Freddie dug her notebook PC out of her bag and charged it up. Stephanie was busy with her pictures and it seemed as good a time as any to revise the chapter on sea creatures. She found herself much too easily distracted and curious about what Stephanie was doing.

"I don't mean to sound ignorant, but can you explain to me what it is you're doing? It looks pretty interesting."

Stephanie grinned. "If my high school geometry teacher is still alive, she is laughing her ass off over this, or, if she's no longer with us, she's surely spinning in her grave. I was the kid who couldn't master squat in geometry class. I actually looked it up in the dictionary and asked why I even had to learn about the goddamn 'study of the measure of the Earth,' anyhow! Most of this is done by computer nowadays, but sometimes I have to be the computer, and this is pure unadulterated geometry."

Stephanie held both index fingers and thumbs out in L-shapes to indicate a frame. "These are the angles of your picture. As long as you zoom in and out with them still in proportion to one another, you can change the degrees and get them to fit in the space that the book allows for." Stephanie then showed Freddie an actual example from the book.

"You're so talented," Freddie whispered.

Stephanie gulped. "Just when I was starting to think I could be in the same room with you and actually concentrate on something else…"

They both agreed it was time for a break.

*   *   *

Their trip up to the visitor center had been spectacular. The sun was setting, and driving higher and higher to the 9300-foot elevation seemed to expand the number of minutes that golden bursts of lights turned to purple haze among the clouds. They had a thermos of pure Kona coffee and a hotpot with cream of tomato soup in the car.

Stephanie had sent Freddie shopping for an additional thermos and Freddie had returned with a fancy, 2.6-liter Japanese Airpot that she'd found on sale for $65. Stephanie had deemed it a terrible extravagance, and when Freddie reacted in horror, she spent several minutes backtracking and extracting her foot from her mouth. It dawned on her somewhat after the fact that Freddie buying things for the house was a step in the desired direction.

Darkness was beginning to surround them as they stood and waited for the rest of their party and nature's nightly star show. Freddie shivered and pulled her hands up into the sleeve of the sweatshirt she had borrowed from Stephanie so that they were protected from the elements. "I had no idea anywhere in Hawaii could be so cold!"

"It's even colder in the winter," Stephanie advised her, wrapping her arms around Freddie's shoulders. "Your cousin and those folks went over four thousand feet higher than this. I bet that is even brisker! Oh, look. See that thing that looks like a star, but is cruising horizontally across the sky?"

"Uh-huh."

"That's a satellite."

"Wow. This is gorgeous. Look at all those stars. And I was impressed with what we could see just above town! The moon is starting to rise, so the sky will get lighter and they probably won't be as vivid then."

"I was here for the full moon once. We could still see lots of stars and they changed the lens on that big telescope over there and let us view the craters on the moon. So, Professor, will the three-quarter moon that's coming up give us enough surface to view?"

"I think it should! To tell the truth, my background is somewhat weaker in astronomy and physics than the life sciences and chemistry, and I haven't been concentrating as well as usual—is it a three-quarter moon?" She lowered her voice slightly. "I remember some light peaking into the room the first night...at your house."

Stephanie smiled at Freddie's shy allusion to their first time together. "Hey, it wasn't until I moved to Hawaii that I realized the moon rises later and later at night depending on its phase. I guess I hadn't been paying much attention for thirty-some-odd years! I did notice it was at three-quarters last night. I don't know how you can keep all those disciplines in your head, anyway. Survey of science for high school students must really keep you on your toes!"

Freddie laughed. "Yeah, well, I can't very well stay just a page ahead of the class when I wrote the book. I can see how it would be fascinating to study the stars in a place like this, though."

Was that a noise in the direction of more permanency, kewpie? Stephanie suddenly felt warmer, despite the chill in the air. "It's a relief to know I'm not the only one having trouble concentrating on my work these days," she whispered huskily.

They were facing north and the light from the ascending moon to their right was still faint. The sky above was capped with innumerable dots of light, but they were so completely shrouded in darkness that the murmuring mass of Japanese tourists fifty yards away blended into the background. Stephanie leaned over and gently nuzzled Freddie's neck.

"Oh, lord, just when I was thinking this moment couldn't get any better." A soft whimper escaped from Freddie's lips. Stephanie spun her around and claimed her mouth.

Not sixty seconds later, over their mutual ragged breathing, Freddie heard the entourage head toward them. She moved to disengage, but not quite soon enough. The voice was unmistakably her cousin's, "See, I told you, we just had to look for a couple of dykes making out."

"Isn't 'dyke' disparaging?" Freddie questioned, in lieu of hello.

"It's a reclaimed word," Nicki offered, shining a flashlight in their direction.

Stephanie used the beam of light to spot, hug, and kiss Wendy and Deb. "This is Freddie," she told them, taking Freddie's hand and pulling her closer.

"I bet they've figured that out, Steph," Freddie said, pushing back her sleeves and shaking their hands.

"How was the summit?" Stephanie asked the group.

"Sunset was breathtaking!" Nicki replied.

Freddie escorted most of the group to Stephanie's car and served coffee and soup. Sue and Deb accepted coffee from Freddie and then they quickly launched into a serious discussion of social services. The two had bonded—Deb was talking about family law in Hawaii from her vantage point as a social worker, while Sue spoke to the issues from the perspective of New York Family Court case law.

Nicki sipped her soup and told Freddie all about their stop at Akaka Falls and the Koa wood handicrafts she'd bought at the Prince Kuhio Mall in Hilo. She and Sue had arranged to spend the night with Wendy and Deb and visit Nani Mau Gardens the following morning.

Stephanie and Wendy stayed behind. Wendy said that she preferred to get some herbal tea, so they went inside the visitor station and helped themselves to water and teabags, stuffing the fee inside the honor box. An old film narrated by Johnny Carson was blaring in the background, offering detailed information about the various projects that went on at the observatory. The two women sat down on a tall wooden bench and spoke over the narration. Most of the other visitors seemed to be out of earshot.

"I only saw her by flashlight, but she's even cuter than how you described her!"

"I wouldn't have thought that possible."

Wendy laughed. "Looks like it's going pretty well."

"I'm making progress. She told her husband they were definitely through last night—and a few hours later, she indicated that she…" Stephanie stopped and scooted back on the bench.

"Come on, Steph, that she what?"

"She told me she loved me."

"Of course she does. She'd be a fool not to."

"I know I haven't paid you to say that, so should I expect a bill in the mail?"

Wendy punched Stephanie's knee playfully. "You know, she had a firm handshake for a little thing—this time it feels right, Steph. I could have told you that Jill would fly away. In my book she was for the birds all along."

Stephanie took a moment and then very softly told Wendy what was weighing on her mind. "We love one another, the attraction is undeniable, but she has an actual career in California. She has a Ph.D., she writes textbooks, and she teaches science in a private high school. She hasn't offered to give all that up, and I haven't asked her to."

"We do have schools here!"

"And you're one of the battle-weary teachers who keeps telling me what a disaster our schools are."

"Things are changing, Steph. We have a whole assortment of experimental schools opening in the near future called Charter Schools. And I'm not a good basis for comparison, because I don't have her kind of credentials. Freddie could get a really good job at a private school like Hawaii Preparatory Academy in Waimea. There are a couple of private schools in Kona these days, too. A lot of the positions that she would qualify for are jobs they recruit for on the Mainland, anyway. I have a strong feeling that the two of you will figure something out."

"This is one of those times where I really hope that those woo-woo psychic powers of yours aren't on the fritz!"

Deb and Sue joined them not two seconds later, and Nicki and Freddie trickled in shortly thereafter. The discussion shifted to other subjects.

Stephanie tuned out the conversation, squeezed her eyes shut and repeated her prayer. She felt closer to divine forces at this advanced altitude and asked, once again, that this be the start of something wonderful and not a fond farewell at ninety-three hundred feet.

Epilogue

THERE WERE VERY FEW CUSTOMERS in the Kona Cantina. Freddie and Steph were sitting in a back booth.

"Could we have another order of nachos, please?" Freddie asked the server.

"I can't believe you want another order of those greasy things. You might as well inject it right into your veins."

"Do I say that when you're gorging on french fries, fuckface?" Freddie scowled.

"All the time, cunt." Stephanie glared back at her. "Did I ever tell you that I almost had Thai food the first night I met you?"

"At least two hundred times. I'm not that lucky, though," Freddie countered.

"Say the word. I'll let you be a three-time loser. Fuck the invitations to our fifth anniversary party. I'll buy everyone pizza. We can toast *my* freedom."

"You're going to buy everyone pizza?"

"Yep!"

"Do you even know where any of the cash cards are?"

"No. That's your department." Stephanie placed her hand over Freddie's.

Freddie shivered. The touch of Stephanie's hand, even after five years, was still almost too much.

"I always forget what a tiger you are. In the back of my mind, I think of you as shy and retiring, not willing to take too much of a risk," Stephanie said huskily.

"What ever gave you the impression that I was shy and retiring? Was it when I slept with you three hours after we were introduced, or when I committed unspeakable acts with you in public places? When was I shy? When I stuck my tongue down your throat? When was I unwilling to take a risk? When I gave up a 4-bedroom Malibu home with a pool to live with you and your dog in a bungalow on this rock?"

"Oh, you poor ting, you got plenny reasons to be miserable!" Stephanie said in her best local dialect. "I don't see you down Kona way with da rest of us workin' stiffs. No. You always up deah, in Kamuela, wit da rich kids in da multi-million dollah science lab," she added, her hand trailing up one leg of Freddie's shorts under the table. Freddie groaned in response to Stephanie's boldness. It had been weeks since she'd groped her under a table.

"Listen to us, Kole. Do you remember when every other word out of us was 'I love you?' 'Pass the butter—Here you go. I love you. I'm taking out the garbage—Don't be long. I love you. Have you seen my reading glasses—They're on the desk. I love you.'"

"That was ages ago, kewpie doll. It was another century, for chrissake. I stored most of my photos in albums rather than electronically back then. I know one thing, though—I still get wet every time I look at you."

"Me, too. I love you, Steph."

"I love you, too. So, baby, has being with a woman been as hard as you feared?"

"I can't imagine my life without you. I still will see someone look at us cross-eyed if I take your hand in public, but I feel like I have the last laugh. I live in paradise and I'm deliriously in love."

"No!"

"It's the truth, I'm afraid."

"For every person that gives us a dirty look, there are several hundred that don't notice us. Two middle-aged women out and about together are amazingly anonymous. If we were two young, body-beautiful hets, for example, I think there would be more interest in why our hands were under a table."

Freddie processed this thought for a second and nodded slowly. "And we'd hardly fit the average person's image of lusty lesbians. The porn movies would lead you to believe that such a creature is very young with long hair and 3-inch fingernails."

"Eoow…" Stephanie shuddered in response. "Our pictures should be in the encyclopedia under 'Lusty…'" Stephanie stopped speaking as the server set the second order of nachos on the table. "… 'Lesbians,'" she concluded, as the waitperson retreated. Stephanie scooped the nachos toward her and started munching.

"I thought you weren't going to eat anymore of this greasy shit. God, you're such an asshole," Freddie chided with a derisive snort.

"Yeah, but I'm *your* asshole, kewpie doll."

"Bet your sweet okole, Kole."

THE END

Shari J. Berman

is a writer, educator, Japanese translator and entrepreneur. Her published short fiction includes the title story in the Alyson anthology, **Wilma Loves Betty** *and other Hilarious Gay and Lesbian Parodies* and "The Y Files" in Alyson's **Dykes with Baggage**. The first chapter of her fourth novel, **I Do,** appears in Robinson's **The Mammoth Book of Lesbian Erotica**. Other short stories appear in **Hot + Bothered 2, Hot + Bothered 3** and **Herotica 7**. Her novels are published in Germany by el!es. Her serial, **"The Selena Stories,"** appeared in the **Visibilities Online** magazine for five years. Shari currently serves as the Editorial Coordinator for Justice House Publishing. The English versions of her other romances, the novelization of Selena, and various short stories, as well as the 2002 parody anthology, **Wishful Thinking**, are forthcoming from JHP.

Other books by
Justice House
Publishing

ACCIDENTAL LOVE, BL Miller

Accidental Love is a captivating story between Rose Grayson, a destitute, lonely, young woman, and Veronica Cartwright, head of a vast family empire and extraordinally rich. What happens when love is based on deception? Can it survive discovering the truth?
0-9677687-1-3 $17.99

THE DEAL, Maggie Ryan

Laura Kasdan is cruising along as the News Director at the number one television station in Dallas. When a momentary lapse of control almost costs her a stellar career, she makes a deal to save her job and keep a promise and moves to a smaller station, where she meets a charismatic reporter who promises to turn her well-ordered world upside down.　　0-9677687-7-2　　$17.99

OF DRAG KINGS AND THE WHEEL OF FATE, Susan Smith

Elvis isn't dead, he's just in Buffalo—and he's a she. When Shakespearean scholar Rosalind meets Taryn, a young drag king, they invoke a karmic cycle that began with recorded history. Is their love strong enough to outwit fate and revise their destiny? *Of Drag Kings and the Wheel of Fate* is passion, mystery, and magic, just as you like it.　0-9677687-8-0 $17.99

JOSIE & REBECCA: THE WESTERN CHRONICLES,
BL Miller & Vada Foster

At the center of this story are two women; one a deadly gunslinger bitter from the injustices of her past, the other a gentle dreamer trying to escape the horrors of the present. Their destinies come together one fateful afternoon when the feared outlaw makes the choice to rescue a young woman in trouble. For her part, Josie Hunter considers the brief encounter at an end once the girl is safe, but Rebecca Cameron has other ideas....
0-9677687-3-X $17.99

HURRICANE WATCH, Melissa Good

Dar and Kerry are back and making their relationship permanent. But an ambitious new colleague threatens to divide them—and out them. He wants Dar's head and her job, and is willing to use Kerry to get it. Can their home life survive the office power play?
0-9677687-6-4 $17.99

LUCIFER RISING, Sharon Bowers

Lucifer Rising is a novel about love and fear. It is the story of fallen DEA angel Jude Lucien and the Miami Herald reporter determined to unearth Jude's secrets. When an apparently happenstance meeting introduces Jude to reporter Liz Gardener, the dark ex-agent is both intrigued and aroused by the young woman. A sniper shot intended for Jude strikes Liz, and the two women are thrown together in a race to discover who is intent on killing her. As their lives become more and more intertwined, Jude finds herself unexpected falling for the reporter, and Liz discovers that the agent-turned-drug-dealer is both more and less than she seems.

In eloquent language, author Sharon Bowers paints a dazzling portrait of a woman driven to the darkest extremes of the human condition-and the journey she makes to cross to the other side.
0-9677687-2-1 $17.99

REDEMPTION, Susanne Beck

Redemption is the story of a young woman who finds out that the best things in life are often found in the last place you'd look for them. Angel is a small-town girl who finds herself trapped within her worst nightmare, a state penitentiary. She finds inner strength, maturity, friendship and love while at the same time giving to others something she thought she'd lost within herself: Hope. It is the story of how Angel rediscovers hope blazing within the piercing blue eyes of an-other inmate, Ice. 0-9677687-5-6 $17.99

SEVERAL DEVILS, K. Simpson

What do you do when you live in the most boring city in America, you hate your job, and you're celibate? Invoke a demon to shake things up, of course. Join Devlin Kerry on her devilishly funny deconstructive tour of guilt, fear, caffeine, and suburbia.
0-9677687-9-9 $14.99

TRISTAINE, Cate Culpepper

Tristaine focuses on the fierce love that develops among strong women facing a common evil. Jesstin is an Amazon from the village of Tristaine who has been imprisoned in the Clinic, a scientific research facility. Brenna, the young medic assigned to monitor Jess's health, becomes increasingly disturbed by the savage punishments her patient endures at the hands of the ambitious scientist Caster, and a bond grows between the two women. The struggle Brenna and Jess face in escaping the Clinic and Caster's determined pursuit deepens the connection between them. When they unite with three of Jess's Amazon sisters, the simple beauty of Tristaine's women-centered culture weaves through the plot, which moves toward a violent confrontation with Caster's posse. 0-9708874-0-X $14.99

TROPICAL STORM, Melissa Good

Tropical Storm... Enter the lives of two captivating characters and their world that hundreds of fans of Melissa Good's writing already know and love. Your heart will be touched by the realism of the story. Your senses will be affected by the electricity, your emotions caught up by the intensity. You will care about these characters before you are far into the story... and you will demand justice be done. 0-9677687-0-5 $17.99

A YEAR IN PARIS, Malaurie Barber

When student Chloe Jones becomes an au pair, all she's looking for is an interesting year abroad in Paris, but she gets more than she bargained for in the mysterious Glairon family. While caring for sweet little Clement, Chloe begins to care a great deal for his beautiful but haunted half sister, Laurence. But not even the most romantic city in the world can help these two when the family's secrets threaten to destroy them all. 0-9708874-1-8 $17.99

ABOVE ALL, HONOR, Radclyffe

Single-minded Secret Service Agent Cameron Roberts has one mission-to guard the daughter of the President of the United States at all cost. Her duty is her life, and is the only thing that keeps her from self-destructing under the unbearable weight of her own deep personal tragedy. She hasn't counted on the fact that Blair Powell, the beautiful, willful First Daughter, will do anything in her power to escape the watchful eyes of her protectors, including seducing the agent in charge. Both women struggle with long-hidden secrets and dark passions as they are forced to confront their growing attraction admist the escalating danger drawing ever closer to Blair.

From the dark shadows of rough trade bars in Greenwich Village to the elite gallaries of Soho. Cameron must balance duty with desire and, ultimately, she must chose between love and honor.   0-9708874-1-8 $17.99

BLOOD SCENT, Patty G. Henderson

A story of obsession...

Love beyond the grave.

Blood Scent takes the popular trappings of vampirism, romance and the gothic; bringing them together in a modern tale of a young woman's journey into the dark side of her soul.

Set in fictional Bayton Isle, off the coast of Maine, Samantha Barnes, a successful cover artist for romance novels, must come to terms with her manic depressive past and her obsessive desire to find true love even if it leads her to the grave itself.

When Samantha suddenly finds herself attracted to a woman with a mysterious and haunting past, she is whisked into a nightmare world of vampires, blood and murder. Thinking that she has finally found the perfect lover in Lara Karnov, the unholy pact she forges with the vampire nearly costs her the lives of those who love her most.

Samantha slowly discovers that the infamous Karnov Family is a savvy group of vampires surviving for centuries on the blood of those who served them. By the time Samantha comes to realize the truth, the trail of blood has taken a deadly turn.

The Countess Lara Karnov brings to vampire lore a new and surprising twist in an ending that will haunt you long after you've put the book down.

Blood Scent delivers a bold and daring look into our own darkest fears.   0-9708874-4-2 $14.99

Join the legacy of
Justice House Publishing

☐ ABOVE ALL, HONOR, Radclyffe
0-9708874-2-6 $17.99

☐ ACCIDENTAL LOVE, BL Miller   0-9677687-1-3 $17.99

☐ BLOOD SCENT, Patty G. Henderson
0-9708874-4-2 $14.99

☐ THE DEAL, Maggie Ryan   0-9677687-7-2 $17.99

☐ OF DRAG KINGS AND THE WHEEL OF FATE, Susan Smith 0-9677687-8-0 $17.99

☐ JOSIE & REBECCA: THE WESTERN CHRONICLES,
BL Miller & Vada Foster   0-9677687-3-X $17.99

☐ KONA DREAMS, Shari J. Berman   0-9708874-8-5 $17.99

☐ HURRICANE WATCH, Melissa Good
0-9677687-6-4 $17.99
(Dar & Kerry Vol. 2, the sequel to TROPICAL STORM)

☐ LUCIFER RISING, Sharon Bowers 0-9677687-2-1 $17.99

☐ REDEMPTION, Susanne Beck 0-9677687-5-6 $17.99

☐ SEVERAL DEVILS, K. Simpson   0-9677687-9-9 $14.99

☐ TRISTAINE, Cate Culpepper   0-9708874-0-X $14.99

☐ TROPICAL STORM, Melissa Good 0-9677687-0-5 $17.99

☐ A YEAR IN PARIS, Malaurie Barber 0-9708874-4-2 $17.99

To order by mail send this page and a check or money order for the cover price(s) and $4.95 s/h for the first book (plus an additionall $1 per each additional title) to
Justice House Publishing (JHP), 3902 South 56th St, Tacoma, WA 98409. Delivery can take up to 6 weeks.

Name: _____

Street Address: _____

_____

City/State/Zip: _____

_____

Country: _____

Phone: _____

Email: _____

I have enclosed a check or money order in the amount of

$ _____

Please be sure to check the books you would like to order on the other side of this page.

Visit us on-line at www.justicehouse.com

Order our books at your local bookstore.